Ways of Coping

A collection of 15 stories by

Fleur Speakman

Summer 2020

Contents:

For Colin, Lydia and Dorian

INTRODUCTION

Introduction

This is a collection of short stories where each of the characters has to contend with some kind of dilemma. The settings vary from early Quakerism in the Dales, to Georgian England, through to Jersey under invasion, as well as more recent contemporary scenes. Inspiration came from a variety of sources: the premises of an old Quaker chapel still in use, an unfinished portrait, some research on a historical Georgian female entrepreneur, one or two arresting sculptures, a striking photo of post-war children clambering on a ruined house, a celebrated eighteenth century German monarch famed for his reforms and a series of special tapestries in St Helier in the Channel Islands.

How each character tries to find their way, is the crux of every story.

Fleur Speakman, June 2020

1 BROTHERLY LOVE

We two, my brother Bert and I, were working together in our potato fields on a rather warm day on the island. "Can't you hold that bloody hoe properly, Joe, you daft bastard? Put your back into it for once, arsehole!" he shouted. I forgot how easy it is to rile my older brother by answering back. I'd had enough. My temper flared at what was a fairly constant grumble at my laziness. "You're always getting at me, you bugger," I shouted while Bert took a swing at me with his clenched fist.

Gasping with pain, I yelled, "You're a filthy brute, a swine. No wonder you haven't got a girlfriend." Bert's face crimsoned with fury as he grabbed my arm and twisted it so hard it really hurt, "At least I keep away from jerrybags like that Gloria you think the sun shines out of," he spat out. As I hobbled away with a throbbing arm, my face still stinging from his blow, raging at the scene, I thought of Gloria Jeffries, the girl with film-star looks and a waterfall of dark hair... well out of my teenage league! Course I knew Gloria was only a dream, half the island was in love with her. But a *jerrybag* was the worst thing you could call a woman then. It was a name for someone who went around with the Germans who were occupying our island. I would get even with my brother for that insult and his various punches and other bits of torture, even though he was several years older and heavier than me.

The early years of the Occupation were a bit different from those later on. We even had the odd football match or two against the Germans, each side winning a match, so honours were even. The Jerries even gave some of the younger children rides on their lorries. We heard they were missing their own children. But several bits of our property were confiscated like radios and newspapers. Cars and horses were requisitioned and there were all sorts of other restrictions. Children had to learn German in school which actually wasn't too bad. But after a few years the shortages started. As time went on, food

BROTHERLY LOVE

became in short supply, even the Germans felt the pinch. The Red Cross managed to send each household some food parcels in late 1944 to 1945. Though we were generally all right on the farm as we had some chickens and grew fruit and vegetables. Mum could do some amazing dishes with the Jersey Royal potatoes anyway. But coal had some time back began to run short, quite serious when winter began to bite. People had real difficulty replacing their shoes too, with some children even going barefoot. One boy wore some shoes his dad had made out of an inner tube. People just had to keep wearing their clothes as long as possible. We were totally cut off from the mainland and we even ran out of films to watch and had to keep re-running the old ones for a bit of entertainment.

My father was the strict type: honest, upright, hard-working, but he had increasingly certain days when his rheumatism was really bad. My mother just supported whatever he said and somehow managed to keep the household going. The black market flourished, but people now took to writing anonymous letters to the German authorities telling them about various hidden supplies, hoping to curry favour or pay off old scores. This usually meant a spell in prison on the island if you were caught. But there was one case, when someone was found reading a leaflet from England that had been dropped over the island. Their punishment was to be shipped across to Germany and be stuck in a concentration camp.

One day a German officer appeared at our farm riding a beautiful bay horse, taking care as he jumped down to avoid dirtying his highly polished boots. I noticed an ordinary German soldier with him, driving a small cart which also pulled up at our farm. The officer started making an enquiry about some hidden coal. My father who happened to be having one of his bad days for rheumatism was unable to get out of his chair, but was furious that such a theft was suspected, "Sir, I would never put my family in danger in this way by hiding extra coal or anything else."

3

BROTHERLY LOVE

"Lifting coal sacks is not so good for the rheumatism, eh?" said the officer with a pleasant smile, leaving my father even more speechless with rage. Joan, my mother, with her dainty build and real anxiety for her husband, was, the officer decided after a quick question, unlikely to spend her time heaving around heavy sacks of coal. I, who looked younger and smaller than my nearly fifteen years, had long ago perfected a look which often made my teacher call out, "Joseph Grosmont, are you still with us?" The officer briefly questioned me too, but then gave up as I stuttered and looked blank. Poor Bert now seemed the most likely culprit for that coal business.

The officer pulled out a letter which he read to us. *Extra coal hidden in old hut in Grosmont Farm: A Well-wisher.* Bert when questioned in turn, didn't deny the charge. He took them to the hut where they found the hidden coal which was swiftly put into the cart. Bert was taken off in handcuffs to what we believed would be prison on the island for a couple of weeks or so, or at the most a month. Bad enough, but these were not normal times. "Someone knew about the coal and denounced us," said my father, still very angry with Bert. "Perhaps it was someone who had actually traded the coal with him," ventured my mother. We were not to know at that stage that we would never see Bert again.

Just before he went, the German officer said they would send a couple of their Slav prisoners who were used to farm work to help keep our farm running properly as he understood we would be harvesting the potatoes shortly. We knew of course where most of our harvest would be going. "There is one good thing," said the officer, smiling thinly, "You don't have to pay these slaves any wages!" We had been shocked enough already, and now stared helplessly at each other. Did he mean "slaves" or had he meant to say "Slavs"?

But there was to be no end to the nightmare. As we later discovered, new regulations were now in place. In an attempt to cope with dwindling supplies, punishments for those caught out had become more severe and Bert was shipped off to prison in Germany. I think it was a place called Wurzbach, but in the event we weren't able to make any contact. No news of him filtered through. Even after the Liberation in 1945, he still didn't reappear. Was he still alive? Had he tried to escape? Perhaps he couldn't get back? Frantic letters were written to the Red Cross who eventually discovered about three years later that Bert had been moved to a different German prison and died there of ill-treatment. No further details were supplied.

My parents were desolated. Their eldest son had been the reliable one on whom all their hopes for the future were built. I did my best and vowed to be someone who would learn to run things as efficiently as possible, listening intently to my father's advice as he grew steadily more infirm. The past weighed on me terribly, I had constant nightmares and often dreaded going to sleep. It was a long agony.

One day, it was in 1958, the farm was doing well, and I had just seen a recent advertisement in the town that bus drivers were wanted on the island as drivers were scarce. The wages seemed to be quite good and it seemed like a new opportunity to mix more with people and to get to know the island better. I had learned to drive with an old second-hand car, but I knew I would need proper training. It would do me good and get me out of the rut. There was another reason, I had begun to drink rather more than was good for me over the years, so a job like that should help to keep me straight or I'd be finished. I knew my neighbour who farmed nearby was keen to make me an offer for our farmland and buildings, which I had told him I might consider.

It was at this point that Ellen walked into my life. She had come to buy some eggs from our farm as she was passing and smiled at me, looking at me with her beautiful dark eyes. We chatted as I got out the eggs and then I asked her to come and look at the various kinds of fruit and vegetables that were growing outside, really in order to prolong things. My drab humdrum life had suddenly burst into full glorious technicolour as we walked down some of the rows. A further meeting was arranged and for the first time in years I felt really happy. After that we met quite frequently and one June day, we took a walk along the cliffs close to clumps of wildflowers. Ellen settled herself down, leaning on her elbow near a bank of golden rock roses and stroked my curly hair. "Now Joe, why does a handsome young man like you, out with his girl, often seem to have dark shadows hovering over his life? I'm a bit worried about you."

I'd been waiting for this moment for quite a long time and I was really scared that I would risk everything. "Ellen, do you remember that I once described to you a terrible row I had with my brother years ago, during the Occupation, and then shortly afterwards the Gestapo coming to take him away?" She nodded. "Well, I knew about the hidden coal. I went to that old broken-down shed of ours to look for a mislaid tool a few days after that terrible row we'd had. I was still seething with rage, I just wanted Bert out of the way for a while, so I wrote that anonymous letter. The result was I ruined my parents' last few years by my stupid, thoughtless, cruel act. Worse still, I sent poor Bert to his terrible fate and have been in hell ever since. Believe me, I've often wanted to own up, give myself –up to the police or the law... I imagine it's the end for you and me. Who wants to consort with a war criminal?"

Ellen said nothing for a while, then gave me a big hug while I tried hard to suppress my shaking body from letting out some racking sobs. I was so ashamed, but I couldn't really help myself.

"There's a lot that can be said," Ellen finally responded, "But now is not the right time. You can never forget that past nor should you. But you should think too about the happier times you must have had as a family. But just keep *this* in mind, I'll be there for you. *I'm* not going anywhere."

I knew I didn't deserve happiness, but the relief was indescribable.

2 *SEMPER DIGNITAS*

The Council Chamber was fitted out in dark polished wood with a series of comfortable chairs and tables in an oval formation, and a central, more imposing seat for the Leader of the Council. Up above was a gallery for members of the public and some high windows which gave a filtered light. On one wall a large, rather elegant clock with a starburst surround seemed to emphasise the passing of time. Directly facing it on the opposite wall, the town's colourful coat of arms, complete with Latin motto, *Semper Dignitas*, was confidently inscribed. The translation from the Latin, which we all knew, suggested 'always fit for office' or alternatively 'always dignified'.

Jonathan Davies, the Leader of the Council, checked that all his council members had arrived. Most had, though Vincent, poor chap, was still in hospital with pneumonia. He as Leader was expecting a rather bumpy ride in this committee meeting as he thought of the one item on the agenda which could cause real controversy. As usual the first quarter of an hour allowed members of the public to raise some issues that concerned them. The thin-faced man leaning well forward, seemed pre-occupied with parking problems. He complained with some bitterness that market stallholders were taking up too much of the main street and what were the Council going to do about it? A woman swathed in scarves and wearing a dark furry hat, said she was disgusted that the central public conveniences in the town were now shut and the ones at the other end were often in a terrible unsatisfactory state. Then a nervous-looking lady with a slight stammer, complained about the lack of adequate street lighting in the road she lived in and so it went on for the full quarter of an hour allotted. Notes were made and responses given and then after a reminder that the rest of this particular meeting would be held rather unusually behind closed doors so that the council's views could be freely expressed, the public in the gallery and the lone reporter were ushered out.

Jonathan knew he would be looking forward to one thing after a potentially fraught meeting – a cup of tea with his wife, probably giving her an edited version of any happenings. However, he was tempted also by the thought of that new pale ale Lindale Blonde he had lately discovered. Perhaps a quick half before home as he usually went for a pint afterwards with some of his team. His ear had already been bent so to speak, by emails, phone calls and even texts, after the agenda and various supporting documents had been sent out. The main item had of course been planning permission for the development of Repton Springs, an application put forward by Agran Holdings. The Springs was an area to the west which had become a nature reserve, inhabited by a quantity of rarer birdlife and some interesting insect life. It was cared for by an environmental group on a long lease. A more extensive section was a pleasant recreation area for the town's inhabitants with a number of woodland paths and one or two natural pools and springs. But the final section which had had a more open landscape and was also fairly extensive, had already been sold off by a cash-strapped former council as rough grazing land. It was this third area that had to be considered, though Hugh, his deputy, had pointed out privately, that if permission was granted for the current application, Agran Holdings might well make a case later for obtaining some additional land for even more housing. The current application without the official jargon, cited a critical need for a quantity of two to three-bedroom semis, and included some social housing in the plan. But more crucially, there should be sufficient space for a rather grand hotel with its own golf course.

Jonathan knew that the committee would be really divided as to whether to give Agran Holdings the go-ahead. At the previous council meeting a quick briefing note had already made a summary of the key points towards the close of that meeting. The whole area of Repton Springs had originally been the bequest of an enlightened Victorian benefactor and strictly speaking, the townspeople had already lost part of their facility via the previous sell-off. The nature reserve had improved the area as it was well managed, but others saw it more as a loss of territory. Nevertheless, the nature reserve was a very popular area with the public and the woodland area even more so. Some, though, were convinced that if the Agran Holdings' planning application was successful, it would impact on the nature reserve with increased noise and pollution, and even to some extent have a detrimental effect on the recreational aspect of Repton Springs woodland.

Councillor Clem Blenkinsop, a thick-set pompous man, with a fluent tongue, and essentially a successful businessman, was vehemently in favour of the Agran application, saying, "It's a positive thing for the town. We haven't got a first-rate hotel with its own golf course – just imagine the number of extra visitors that would generate!"

"Jobs! tourism!" chipped in Laurie Fisher who often acted as chorus to Clem's pronouncements.

Hope Clarke, who was generally regarded as a shrewd and sensible woman, asked, "If I may, aren't you forgetting something Councillor Blenkinsop? What about the access to this desirable site? I seem to remember that it's more like a dirt track than a road!"

"Rubbish!" thundered Clem, "that's utter exaggeration. A decent road or two can and ought to be built."

"Who's going to pay for that?" demanded a voice in ringing tones, while Sally Birkin interrupted," Nobody seems to have noticed the 'sweetener' that was offered." There was a pause as the council considered what she might be referring to. "I mean that on the application there was a site for a number of houses **and** eight houses designated as social housing. But who would want to live up there with no facilities?"

"There's a bus calls nearby Tuesdays and Saturdays," – this from someone who hadn't spoken so far.

"Yes, very useful, about three-quarters of a mile away and what about its frequency?" demanded Sally.

"What we haven't taken into account, is the disruption to the birds and other wild-life, and the increased pollution from the traffic. Think of the air quality." This was Hope again, a great botanist and keen ornithologist.

"A bleeding-heart environmentalist!" raged Clem, turning to his acolytes, who nodded in agreement. "So, these creatures matter more than giving people homes!" he thundered, turning red with repressed fury.

"There is no need for rudeness," retorted Hope, who could be thoroughly aroused when a cause was dear to her heart. "Pollution, air quality is really significant, a serious matter, causing respiratory diseases even death in some cases!"

"That hotel and golf course will bring in increased trade to the town. It's good for the town's economy, "insisted Clem. "They'll find the money for some decent roads too."

"Who do you mean by 'they'? The Highways Authority?" queried a member who rarely spoke.

"Anyway, people will get lifts, be neighbourly for a change," was Norman's suggestion, in an attempt to quieten things down. But Clem who genuinely believed in public service and whose hardware store was famed for helping its customers from the uncertain novice to the more sophisticated DIY-er, pressed on. "I was talking about increased employment prospects, increased prosperity and desirable accommodation. It seems to me we are forgetting that the townspeople are expecting a mature well-thought out decision, not just some frivolous remarks from some of our fellow council members here."

Now as Leader of the Council, I felt I had to intervene. "We have today listened to a number of what are obviously a variety of strongly felt views and all shades of opinion. Any decision we make will not be an easy one. I would suggest we arrange to hold a public meeting in the town hall in the near future to which Agran Holdings and the Nature Reserve people are invited, I am happy to represent our Council as Leader, or nominate my deputy, Hugh Martins, if the Council prefer this. But we must also have a neutral chairman. In addition, we might ask a local transport group to help us examine the issue of potential private and public transport as well as the road problem at Repton Springs. The public will then be given the opportunity to ask their questions. This will just give us time at the next council meeting for a vote and a definitive decision on this planning application."

But Clem, still looking furious, pompously gathered up his papers with great deliberation and stalked majestically towards the door. Unfortunately, he lost his bearings a little. Mistaking the nearest door for the exit from the chamber, he wrenched it open and closed it with a bang, finding himself suddenly in a totally dark walk-in cupboard, as we all knew. There was a breathless hush as the clashing of buckets and mops and what were probably muffled expletives were heard. This seemed to go on for several seconds. I was about to send out a rescue party, when Clem emerged, looking dishevelled and even angrier, muttering hoarsely "wrong door" before disappearing into the night.

"*Semper Dignitas!*" said Hope with a bright smile as we all collapsed into rather unseemly laughter.

3 AN EVENTFUL DAY

"Are you accusing me of being a wife-beater?" The well-dressed rather self-confident man, probably in his late forties, seemed amused as he sat back in his chair.

But the two men seated opposite both felt there had been a sort of controlled aggression behind his statement, when they discussed matters afterwards. Morris, the Detective Inspector, answered, "We did not pose any such question, Mr Lofthouse. We were merely asking you to help us shed some light on Mrs Lofthouse's recent serious accident. You agreed to do so. As you had already left the hospital, we came to talk to you at home. We assumed that you would be happy to help us with our enquiries. We can understand this has been a very difficult day for you. But if you can give us some indication of what time you returned from the office and what your wife was doing at that point, it would be much appreciated."

Peter Lofthouse sighed theatrically. He said there had been only two of them in the house as far as he knew, when he came home shortly after 4.30pm straight after a board meeting. He explained that he had run upstairs to fetch a book and then found his wife in their bedroom looking somewhat annoyed as he had forgotten to put his dirty washing in the laundry basket and had left it scattered round the bedroom. They had started arguing over this quite trivial matter, a bit heatedly, and then she stormed off, catching her foot on a large ornamental vase near the top of the stairs and had fallen headlong to the bottom. She had lain there in a crumpled heap, obviously in great pain. Of course, he had rushed down, realising she must be badly hurt, and immediately phoned for an ambulance. In his distress he had inadvertently led the operator to believe there might have been an intruder. When the ambulance crew arrived, he had followed his wife to hospital in his own car as instructed and was later told that her injuries were deemed to be critical. He was then asked to return home and phone the

13

hospital later in the evening. The DI thanked him again and said they would be in touch, while his colleague Detective Sergeant Manners put away his few notes. They both stopped at the bottom of the stairs as they passed and looked upwards at the rather heavy ornamental vase near the top of the stairs before they left the house.

"Well, Manners what's your view? "queried the DI, "about this accident?"

"I don't think he's telling us everything," responded his colleague, cautiously.

"So!" exclaimed "his boss, "it's a hell'uva row about some laundry, however house-proud you are. It was probably about something rather different. But was she pushed, or did she really trip over something?"

Manners who was no 'yes' man, replied cautiously, "To be fair sir, people can argue about trivialities and then it all blows out of proportion. By the way, it's interesting that that heavy vase apparently didn't topple over."

Morris's mobile beeped and he listened carefully before thanking the caller. "That was the hospital about Sheila Lofthouse. She has very serious internal injuries, some of these appear to be inconsistent with a fall. Although she did have a fall as well but after an attack. They said it appeared she had been used, in layman's terms, as a 'punchbag'. The two officers stared at each other and looked grave. There was now plenty of work to be done by the whole team: forensics would be photographing and dusting for prints, interviews would have to be set up with friends, relatives, neighbours, and with key staff at both the husband's and wife's place of work – and that was just for starters.

AN EVENTFUL DAY

"What about that intruder, sir? Perhaps forensics could check for extra prints and if that person really existed, perhaps some neighbour saw something."

"Good thinking," answered the DI, clapping Manners approvingly on the back. "We can't rule it out completely. However, our friend Lofthouse could be deliberately muddying the waters. There's another thing: we'll need to check if Lofthouse has previous. Is he on our database for any reason or has his wife ever been in hospital with some injury which might have been the result of domestic abuse? Or has she ever reported such a matter to us and then withdrawn her complaint?"

My day had started rather badly and got worse. There was a new chit at the office. Sonia in Finance, rather good knockers on her and a certain way of swaying her hips. I'm convinced she'd brushed past me on purpose the other day with a smile and an expression that seemed to imply, "I'm up for it!" So, I pop down to Finance this morning with some figures in a folder and catch sight of her with that ghastly Marcia from Human Resources at the water cooler. I manage not be seen by slipping behind some free-standing display material, hoping that Marcia will soon disappear.

Then I overhear part of their conversation... That bitch of a Sonia was just saying, "Oh, they'll do anything to get you in the sack. Thing is, it's usually these older men who think they're god's gift like that chap upstairs. Pathetic! Isn't he about number three in the firm's pecking order?" Marcia laughed and agreed as they started to go off together. I deliberately became visible, greeted both ladies warmly, who looked rather uncomfortable, and went back upstairs, inwardly seething with fury.

AN EVENTFUL DAY

At the board meeting, the boss looked thoroughly out of humour. It turned out our sales figures for this quarter and the one before were well down and he decided that I was the chief culprit. He claimed it was my advice that had caused some very adverse decisions. When I attempted to suggest that decisions always had a joint or common responsibility, he decided to use sarcasm. To be blunt, he made me look a complete fool in front of the whole Board. My teeth were now thoroughly on edge and I controlled myself with difficulty. I resolved as soon as the meeting was over, I would return home early and try to find some solace.

Back at home I was surprised to find Sheila bustling around upstairs. It turned out that there had been a small fire where she worked and as there was no power, staff had been given the afternoon off till it was all sorted out. I was hoping for peace and quiet, but then she rounded on me, confronting me with what she called my pornographic magazines she had found in my study. I told her she had no right to meddle with my private affairs whereupon she worked herself up, calling me all the names under the sun, including 'a fucking pervert'. I saw red and told her to stop, but she refused. Normally she avoids confrontation and would have stopped in her tracks, careful not to push it. But today she was like a fury. I couldn't stand any more and took a swing at her while she still taunted me.

"I'll stop your fucking noise once and for all," I yelled as she lay on the ground and pummelled her repeatedly with my fists. I may have even given her the odd kick. She lay there motionless for a while. Then I stopped and watched as she crawled painfully away. It gave me a strange sense of power. I felt I was fighting back against all of them. She finally managed to get by inches to the top of the stairs and hesitated as if unsure which way to go. Suddenly a voice inside my head whispered insistently, "You ought to help her down, the quick way."

AN EVENTFUL DAY

Why not? I thought a little push and it's all over. Could I do it? She saw me coming and I saw real hatred in her eyes. Right!... just that little push and over she toppled with the most frightful bang of a heavy object falling... falling. I was now shaking with terror. What on earth had possessed me? Had I been totally mad? I approached her carefully but couldn't really look at her. Was she dead? I covered her with a light travel rug we kept handy for cold nights and with trembling hands, phoned the emergency number.

4 GROWING PAINS

Stuart woke up with a start. What had jerked him awake? Hilary, his wife, was fast asleep next to him and it felt like the middle of the night. He pondered, found the small bedside alarm clock which had been pointing the wrong way and discovered from its luminous dial it was just after 3 o, clock in the morning. He thrust on his warm dressing gown against the cold, though he had trouble finding one of the sleeves in the dark. After hunting for his slippers, which had somehow gone in different directions, he started to tiptoe across the room.

There seemed to be a chink of light under the door of Olly's bedroom. Had the youngster forgotten to turn out the light or was he feeling unwell? He padded on, worrying a little, and crossed the landing, opening Olly's door a fraction. There was Olly, sitting up in bed, apparently absorbed in operating a device, a black box. He assumed it to be a game of some kind. Relief and amazement chased each other over Stuart's features.

Olly flinched as he saw Stuart enter the room, looking first worried, then a more truculent expression came over his face. Stuart, who had been trying to build a real relationship with his two stepchildren for over a year, had always found them generally polite, but detached. He was now careful to make his voice as neutral as possible and reasonably friendly. "Olly, what would your dad have done if he had found you playing games at three in the morning?" Olly thought for a moment. "He'd have bawled me out, and cuffed me one on the ear as well."

"I see!" said Stuart. "I hope we both agree that's it's not the right time to be using this console, whatever it is. Though it looks like a complicated object. I'd like to know how it works sometime. Was it a present?"

GROWING PAINS

"No, it's really my dad's. But he said I could borrow it for a while if I was careful with it. It's an x-box," said Olly, helpfully."

"But why at this time of the night?"

Well, I couldn't sleep after a while, so I just thought I'd play on it for a bit at first. Then it must have got late," answered Olly, looking carefully at Stuart to see what might be coming next.

"Look, we'd better keep our voices down. Just think of the trouble you could be in." 12-year-old Olly looked distinctly unhappy at this reminder.

"Though I think you must be pretty bright to get this to work." He spotted a look of pleasure on the youngster's face. "But it's really not the right time with school tomorrow. What do you think?"

Olly sighed and started to pack away the console "Don't let my sister Sarah get at it," he begged. "She's always jealous, but not really interested in it." But the youngster's face was still anxious as if something else was bothering him.

"What's worrying you now?" asked Stuart. "It's this horrible French homework. I'm just crap at all that."

"Is it something to hand in or to learn?"

"We've got a load of French vocabulary to learn for a test. It's the day after tomorrow. But I keep thinking about doing really badly. Our teacher said she'd keep people in if we didn't get most of it right."

"Well, we can sort that out. My French isn't too bad, even after all these years. We could give it a go tomorrow if you like." Olly thought for a while. "Well if you really can," he said doubtfully. Then in a rush. "Sarah over-heard something last night on the phone. You were away, getting back late from New York. Mum was talking on the phone to someone. Sarah thought she said my dad was moving away out of the country with his new family."

Stuart realised this would indeed really upset the children as they saw their father, who had a new family, by regular arrangement. It be could true. After his delayed flight, he had had no real time to talk to his wife when he returned. He had been exhausted and she had just gone to sleep after first giving him a big hug.

"One thing at a time Olly. Let's both get some sleep. I'll help with French tomorrow after school and you can give me a lesson on that games console of yours."

Olly yawned and gave a half smile, starting to settle down in bed. "Good night," said Stuart softly as he started to close the door.

A few weeks later Hilary was sorting out some of the kitchen cupboards on a Saturday afternoon, when she heard an object being flung right across a bedroom by the sound of it. It must be Sarah doing something up there in her own room as everyone else was out. Then she heard a sob and a cry of "Bitch, Bitch!" When she came into Sarah's room, she found her 14year old daughter had collapsed into a sobbing heap on the floor. "What on earth has happened?" asked her mother, full of concern. Between gulps and sobs, her daughter pointed to her phone. So at least, thought Hilary, it wasn't her phone that had made that loud clattering noise. It must have been a shoe or something else. She couldn't see what the message on the phone was, but she did wonder who might have sent it."

GROWING PAINS

"It's that..." obviously wanting to spare her mother the word she really wanted to use, Sarah decided on, "That fiend Orla!"

"Isn't Orla your best, best friend?"

"Huh! She was supposed to be. She's now spreading lies about me because she thinks Gareth Morgan rather likes me and that bitch wants him for herself. He's great!"

"I think you should ignore it. If you don't answer, perhaps those texts or messages will stop."

"You don't understand. It'll be on Twitter and the rest, all sorts of lies about me, really nasty."

"But people who really know you won't believe them. Is this boy Gareth someone in your year?"

"No. But he smiles when he sees me. He's two years above me. He's cool."

"Come downstairs and have a cup of coffee. I've some homemade flapjacks, and you can tell me some more if you want to."

"I don't want to. I'm not hungry. Anyway grownups (this was said with a real sneer) lie to their children anyway or leave out information."

"What do you mean by that?"

"I overheard you some time ago on the phone, talking, probably to a friend, when our stepdad was away. It sounded as if our real dad was going to move abroad."

"Oh, I remember now. I was talking to my mother, your gran, In fact. The move, it's only a possibility, nothing's definite. We would have told you if it was. Denmark was mentioned."

GROWING PAINS

"There you are! My best friend hates me, my real father doesn't want to know me, he's only interested in his new family, and you and Stuart gang up against Olly and me. Anyway, I don't want to go to that stupid effing show you've got tickets for. It sounds crass."

"Oh, that's a real shame! Gran's coming as well. She's really looking forward to Kinky Boots."

"Is she really? My gran's going to that musical?"

Sarah who was very fond of her Gran, had stopped in her tracks.

"She'll be very disappointed if you decide not to go. She's coming here, as it happens, in a few minutes, as she wanted to show us something special."

Sarah who felt really deflated after her tantrum, felt intrigued in spite of herself, and wondered what it could be.

By the time her grandmother had arrived, she was on hand to look at the large rather heavy parcel she carried. Gran asked for the table to be extended and pulled out something unexpected. It was a large heap of fabric which she spread right across the table. There it was, the most beautiful shimmering peacock with tail spread and head held proudly aloft as the huge central motif of a large patchwork quilt. Delicate embroidery had enhanced the effect. The bird's feathers seemed to almost quiver in their delicacy.

"Gran," breathed Sarah. "That's absolutely gorgeous! The work in that!"

"Congratulations! Mum! You could put that in an exhibition," said Hilary in awe of her mother's achievement. "Look at that intricate pattern as well on that edging. It looks like those Spanish tiles."

"Well, as a matter of fact, my quilt has just been accepted for the Quilt Museum in town. They are mounting a new exhibition, though it won't be for a while. I had to send photos, small samples of my work, measurements and all sorts of details. They even sent one of their team to view it. So, I'm very excited about all that. I just wanted to show it to you both, so you'll get the first viewing. They'll finalise dates later."

"Gran, I'd love to do something a bit like that, but smaller like a cushion. Could I?"

"Yes, why not, my love. You can use all sorts of different shapes and colours. You never know, you might start a fashion for it at your school."

Sarah beamed happily. The world seemed suddenly to have become a more interesting place again. "Gran, I'm so glad you're coming with us to that musical show."

5 A PROMISE BROKEN

I always enjoyed visiting my grandmother, listening to stories of her early childhood. She would watch for the horse-drawn milk cart coming up from the farm while her mother would go out with a special jug in her hand. Then the milk, with a slight froth, was poured into the jug from a metal container with a tap, then carried carefully into the house. At times gran used to help her mother pick fruit in the garden to make into jam: gooseberries glowing red and rather special, wonderfully sweet and good to eat, or the more tart-tasting red and black currants. She would watch her mother skilfully making her cakes without weighing anything, while she was allowed to add raisins or cocoa powder, her special job being to rub the cake tins with an old butter paper.

As I grew a little older, I became fascinated with some of the things in gran's house, lovely little boxes, crystal vases, a rather pretty pottery figure and later some of the paintings on the walls. There was one particular painting called *The Letter*. I used to make up stories about the young girl in the picture in her violet dress, standing there in a lovely garden reading that letter. Was it good or bad news? Had a friend written or was it from a young man she loved, telling her how much she meant to him? Was he going away to seek his fortune, explaining that they would be apart for some time? Or was he going away for ever? Maybe the letter told of a serious illness about someone close to her or even the news of some terrible tragedy. Gran believed the picture was painted in Victorian times, she'd said, looking at what the girl wore and her kind of hairstyle. But she couldn't ever find the artist's signature or even a date. I helped her once look very carefully. We even took the painting off the wall and checked the back of it. I loved that picture, the sunny garden, the girl slightly turned away. It was a sort of satisfying puzzle. Sometimes I felt there was a slight droop to her shoulders, at others, she looked as if she was savouring something special. I also began to appreciate the way some of the folds in her dress were high-lighted, and the way the light caught her reddish hair and the fresh green of the leaves and grass. At some stage Gran said that she would put something in her will about me having that picture, since I liked it so much. I desperately hoped that day was very far off. Yet it would in time be a rather special memory and some sort of consolation after losing someone so very dear to me.

I was by far the youngest of three children. Laurence and Serena were grown up, earning their living very successfully in our firm's glassworks. Reynolds' Glass was quite an important local employer and had a good reputation generally. Laurence was already in quite a senior position, idolised by my mother and sister for his blond good looks and charm. I thought it more significant that my father rated Laurence's business abilities pretty highly. More recently my father had spent more of his time travelling abroad, looking for new outlets and observing new techniques at special exhibitions, so he was not so often at home. My sister Serena was one of the firm's design team. Everyone said she was very creative and apparently in the running for some award or other. My mother worked part-time in the business, dealing mainly with customer relations and some publicity matters. Although I was still only fifteen, with GCSE looming, fond as I was of my family, I knew I really didn't want to work for our firm. I wanted the chance to work as a curator in a major art gallery or museum as I had become interested in different types of art and was keen on finding out more about various civilisations and artefacts. The trouble was, with such an age gap between the three of us, I was seen as the baby of the family and treated either as a pet or a nuisance, according to whim or so it seemed to me. No one had really noticed who I was, my mother seeing anyone in their teens, me included at times, as one of a strange tribe of 'terrible teens'.

Around this time my grandmother started to have some occasional health problems. One day she was taken to hospital suffering from pneumonia, with some other complications. The shock when she died was shattering. I couldn't really find words for how I felt. I wandered round dazed and disbelieving, convinced I would somehow catch a glimpse of her somewhere. The family insisted on a traditional church service which I was not sure was something she would really have wanted, but of course I had no say in the matter.

At the time appointed, all the close family gathered to hear her last will and testament. There were various bequests and a very generous sum of money to each of us, her three grandchildren; mine was actually larger; as according to her, I had yet to make my way in the world. The rest of the estate as it was called, was left unconditionally to my mother, her daughter, including the house and its contents. The two executors were, of course, my mother and my brother, as the eldest grandchild.

At this point I remembered the painting I loved and tried to pluck up courage to ask the solicitor hesitantly if a special painting had been mentioned in the will. The solicitor frowned and paused, speaking weightily, while my family stared amazed as if a footstool had come to life and spoken.

"My dear young lady, I can assure you, our client, the late Mrs Evelyn Hughes, was advised by us, as a matter of policy, not to itemise particular objects as there is always the danger of such objects going astray, being damaged or even attracting controversy."

There was no response I could make, but I felt myself seething with rage.

He took his leave shortly afterwards. My sister Serena asked me curiously, "Which painting did you mean?"

A PROMISE BROKEN

"It's the painting called *The Letter* which hung in gran's bedroom. It's Victorian. She loved it and I do too. She *really* said she would put it in her will for me."

"Well, she probably forgot or listened to her solicitor's advice," said my mother briskly.

Lawrence now broke in.

"Victorian, you say. These things are really fashionable at the moment. It could be worth a lot of money, even if it's second division. As executor I ought to take it to be valued by experts." The others nodded in agreement. My face fell, value didn't matter to me.

My brother, the successful businessman, went on, "If it turns out to be really valuable, we three grandchildren should share the proceeds when we sell it." My mother didn't say anything. I felt both fury and utter horror. Seeing my expression, he then said, "Well Fran, you will have a considerable sum of money, according to the bequest we have just heard about. You could have the painting once it's valued and pay Serena and me a third each of that value."

I never knew if he was actually serious. If he was, I thought it was utterly monstrous and callous, and equally so if he was actually teasing me.

My father, with a very serious face, went over to speak to him, but I was very near tears and went out of the room without looking at anybody, knowing I would shortly burst into a storm of weeping.

6 UNFINISHED

A hand grabbed his shoulder and a cheerful voice shouted above the din, "Tom, you young dog, what do you mean by skulking into corners and not advising your friends where you are?"

Before Tom could answer, his fellow artist Ned Richardson, had whipped out his sketch book and with a few quick satirical strokes, had comically exaggerated Tom's features and stooped posture. A second lightning sketch showed Tom's amazement as he was discovered by his friend, his wig apparently slightly awry.

Imperiously waving over one of the coffee house waiters, Ned ordered coffee for himself and a re-fill for his friend. "What news?" he enquired of the old waiter as the coffee was poured out in an aromatic stream. "His gracious majesty, the King, will be driving down the Mall shortly," returned the old waiter.

"Pah! You know better than that Simon. We're after the real stuff – which prominent Whig will defect to the other side or which Tory minister has a new aristocratic mistress? Best of all, which important personage is come to town and wishes to have their portrait painted?"

The old waiter smiled, shaking his head, ready to serve another customer.

"Now Tom," and Ned's more boisterous tones were muted, "how was the desolate North? The only time I was ever in those regions, I still recollect the dank chill. But what of Lord Arnedale and your great painting commission?" Tom's face showed some strong feeling as he said slowly, "My painting will remain unfinished."

UNFINISHED

Ned stared hard at him and said bitingly, "So, having lured you up to those frozen wastes, my lord decides, in his infinite wisdom, that your talents are insufficient for his commission."

"No, you err, that was not so."

Ned's brow furrowed, a sly grin appeared on his face and he waggled an admonishing finger. "Tom! You sly dog!"

"Ned, I can assure you it had nothing whatever to do with me directly. I'll tell you what occurred without making too long a tale. The journey north by coach and cart to Arnedale Hall was somewhat wearisome. The Hall itself is a fine, fashionable, tastefully furnished Palladian establishment, with landscaped grounds and a considerable estate. The young heir, who has an arrogant mien, judging by his portrait painted by Sir Joshua Reynolds no less, was mercifully on the Grand Tour with his tutor in Italy or Greece and would not return for some time. Two younger children, daughters who were eleven and ten, were the subjects of my commission; the particular wish of my Lady Arnedale who was in poor health. She felt that Sir Joshua's style was too dramatic and wanted softer contours and colours".

Ned grinned again, delighted, but he asked, "So you lived at the Hall?"

"I was given a room on an upper floor for my sleeping quarters. A room overlooking the parterre was made available on the ground floor for the sittings. Fortunately, it was airy and well lit. There was also a useful deep closet nearby with a lock, where I could keep all my equipment. I had the freedom of the grounds, was given a tour of the principal rooms and even occasional permission to use the library. I could also escape to the local inn some evenings with local villagers for company or even some of the young bloods of the squirearchy. Yes, I can see the question in your eyes. I was not always successful in my games of hazard."

"But the two daughters Tom? – of course, you have two of your own…"

"The girls came in with a very starchy governess which dismayed me a little. I introduced myself with a slight bow. I knew that my life would be much pleasanter if the governess, a Miss Osbourne, did not see me as a threat to her authority. On the other hand, becoming too confidential could cause problems for me, a happily married man. These large houses, you may not be aware, are a perpetual hotbed of gossip. However, after a week or two, the housekeeper decided I must be a fount of information on London fashions and habits, quizzing me on such subjects and occasionally asking me to drink a dish of tea with her. She used to unlock her supply with great ceremony." His friend shook his head and blew out a small cloud of tobacco from his pipe which joined the rest in the smoke-thickened atmosphere.

"When I was first introduced to the two girls, Maria the eldest and Louisa her younger sister, I saw a close facial likeness which I hoped to bring out in my painting. I explained to Miss Osbourne and the girls that a number of "sittings" would be needed. I hadn't finally decided whether the girls would be standing or seated. I told them it was always called a "sitting" even if I actually painted them standing up. Miss Osbourne, who had occupied herself at one side of the room with some fancywork, remarked to the girls with a smile, "You are now sitting for your sitting," as after some preliminary rough sketches, I decided on a seated position. The two young misses were delighted at her wit, giggling in appreciation. They then glanced a little apprehensively at me, but I smiled back good-humouredly.

UNFINISHED

"Our sittings progressed. Maria and Louisa were both arrayed in fine white dresses, the elder who had fairer hair, had a knot of sky-blue ribbon on her dress, while the younger with slightly darker curls, wore a pink one. I felt a little constrained by the traditional full-face style that is the fashion for portraits. The two sisters were genuinely fond of one another, as I saw, at one point, Maria put a protective arm around Louisa. I now really had my pose. I asked them to look up as if something had attracted their attention. Maria looked very faintly amused and thoughtful. Louisa, who had a merry temperament, I discovered, also had occasionally a slightly wistful air. I was keen to incorporate something of the beauties of the natural world outside and planned to set the girls in a landscape which had elements of their own parkland. There was a splendid uninterrupted view from the pleasure grounds across to the fields where some cattle were grazing. But a woodland nook would better suit my purpose. This I sketched in with light strokes and saved for the more final stages of my work. I concentrated all my energies particularly on their faces. I left further details of their clothing again for later. Our sittings progressed and the young misses who lost some of their shyness, made me think at times fondly of my own two girls." As Tom paused and drank down a draught of his cooling coffee, Ned asked if some particular difficulty had arisen.

Tom's earlier animation vanished. He was now lost in thought. "Louisa was suddenly taken ill with a high fever. The local doctor was sent for, but as her condition worsened, a messenger was even posted to London for more specialist help. The London doctor arrived in his own carriage, setting off as soon as he heard the state of the case, but by then could do little... The funeral was held a few days later. Before I left, Lady Arnedale sent for me and graciously said the unfinished painting would hang in her private quarters and give her some material comfort. I bowed my acknowledgements. She offered me her own hand with great dignity and insistently pressed into it a packet with my remuneration and a tiny keepsake marked

31

UNFINISHED

'Louisa' which of course I could not refuse. I surmised a lock of the poor child's hair. I found it very difficult to master my emotion; a mingling of genuine sadness and real regrets.

7 ALL ON A SUMMER'S DAY

Viewed from Swindale Crag above the Dales village of Felton, a large heavy cart was making its laborious way upwards from the nearby market town in the valley.

I had left my oatcakes to cool. My husband had gone to help a neighbour rebuild a field-wall on an outlying farm in the Upper Dales. There was a dazzling light in the sky and the heat was rising. My friend and neighbour, Hannah, in her airless home, was only a few weeks from bringing her latest into the world... I begged her to come to a cool spot where there was a patch of meadowland full of flowers and a great shady tree. She could rest there, and the two little ones could play quietly nearby. "I'll bring my cloak, Alice," she answered, "to place on the ground 'gainst stinging plants." Anne, nearly three and her brother Walter a year younger, romped gleefully, picking a few field flowers, but quietened when I pointed to their sleeping mother. They nestled next to me, as I told them a story about a cuckoo we had heard calling. I had had seven babies myself and only the twins had survived for a few years. The Lord in his wisdom had taken all of them to a better place. But there was a sore spot round my heart when I thought of their cruel fevers and sufferings. When Hannah awoke, she said she would await her husband's return from the Upper Dales in their cottage. I said I would bring the children to her a little later.

As I approached the village, Old Jack came limping towards me. "Alice, thou hast better make haste to see thy Friend." Scooping up the children in my arms, I heard one of the village curs barking and growling angrily at a stranger. I hastened forward to see a most sorry sight. Three of our elders in their usual sober garb with their wide brimmed hats were seated on straw in a large cart. In the corner furthest from me, I saw a huddled figure and recognised first of all her cloak and the hood, which half-covered her face. My dear friend Hannah struggled to sit upright when she heard little Anne and Walter

33

breaking into loud wails. Putting out her arms to them, she kissed their little faces, while the carter kept his face averted and a person in a new-looking set of buff coloured clothes and hat, with a pistol in his hand, looked impatiently on. To add to my horror and distress, I saw that the elders had shackled hands. The whole scene shocked me deeply. Full of foreboding I asked the buff-suited one where they were going. "York, mistress. York – two day's travel."

"Why?" I demanded, almost knowing the answer. "Them that hold services in their homes or take part in them are fined." He paused for breath, "Can't or won't pay means goods taken or prison." He rocked back on his heels and looked challenging at me. I took him a little to one side.

"Thou art a Christian and a good man. Pray take this coin and look to my friend. See she has some comfort in her time of need," As I spoke, I was pointing to Hannah's unmistakeable shape. He took the coin, but made no answer. We, the Friends, do not use formal titles or even bow our heads or curtsey to anyone. A good-hearted neighbour took the two children and showed them her new kitten, as with a full heart I ran after the cart for a parting look at Hannah. "Pray Alice, succour my children 'gainst my husband 's return." I could hardly speak for dread, but reassured her and smiled, though I knew only a dank prison cell in York Castle gaol awaited her. How could she endure without harm two days' travel on a jolting cart before even reaching York? Someone had come and denounced the Friends... Though the law had changed. We were now licensed to use our Meeting House. Why had only Hannah and the three elders been taken? This was a sore puzzle to me at first.

Then I remembered an event. Once when I was due to report to the elders on some charitable matter, I was struck down by a low fever, losing much weight and sure my end had come. Hannah insisted that she would make my report for me at the home of one of our elders, while an elderly neighbour looked

34

after her children. We are a very close community in Felton. Only a few elders were meeting in Simon Wilkinson's house for some discussion as Hannah made her report and the group sat in silence for a while, then studied a short passage in the Scriptures. As they sat with their Bibles open, there was a soft tap on the outer door. Simon called out "Enter!" and they continued, finishing their readings as a man entered respectfully, with his hat well pulled down over his brows. Simon then continued, "We'll say a short prayer for our dear Friend Alice's recovery." The stranger stood courteously in the shadows till they had finished, then asked his way, mentioning he was on horseback. He gave his name, though Hannah could not recollect it, but his accent was not local, and nobody knew him. As the elders explained his best route, he thanked them all, said he might come again as he was interested in the Friends. "He took out his tablets and asked our names to remember us by. I was the only one," said Hannah, "who thought that somewhat strange. Afterwards I thought he could have been an informer as they call themselves."

I was sure Hannah had guessed correctly. There was a fine if you were deemed to have met illegally for a religious meeting in someone's home. I knew that the fine would be beyond the means of most people even if they wished to pay it. My husband would not have permitted payment even for Hannah. We all had little enough of any value. We were a poor Dales community of mainly small farming folk. The Friends would not even allow someone outside their faith to pay those fines... It was like looking into an abyss...

Parson Joshua Manders is my name, I reside in a comfortable living near York. Part of my occasional duties are to minister unto those of the criminal fraternity in York Castle gaol. Those prisoners who wish to make their peace with God I visit and for some I am virtually the last person they see as their heinous

35

crimes receive the terrible judgement they have so richly merited. It is not a pleasant task to try to bring some comfort to such wretches, who have often had a most miserable existence and insist on narrating much of their history to me. Often, I have had to listen to an incredible catalogue of thievery, villainy and debauchery in cells full of noxious vapours. A week ago, I was asked to undertake one more visit that day to a Quaker, a dying woman. I did so with some reluctance and ever since I have suffered the most tremendous turmoil.

Here is my testimony

Those creatures who call themselves the Friends are an abomination before God. They disobey the laws of church and state, and furthermore are traitors to their King. They totally refuse to swear the oath of allegiance. Indeed, any oath is against their conscience, forsooth. They make their own arrangements for marriages and funerals sacrilegiously and keep their own birth, burial and marriage registers. They even use un-consecrated ground, some small field to bury their dead, but do not mark the details there in a truly Christian manner. To me they are worse than cut-purses or murderous felons since they know full well what they are doing and have some basic education. I have preached many a rousing sermon against them, as some species of devil or demon. How can they presume to study and comment on the holiest of holy, our precious Bible? I have even had my own sermons denounced by this pernicious rabble in my own church and been set upon on at least one occasion by a Quaker mob outside throwing stones.

This woman Hannah had given birth in prison and was very weak. Maybe I could show her the true path of righteousness in her final hours. I believe I have great powers of persuasion.

ALL ON A SUMMER'S DAY

I found her sharing a tiny foetid dark cell with an arrow-slit of day-light, with two slatternly hard-faced females. In fact, she hardly stirred at first as I approached.

The turnkey said her baby had died shortly after birth and added, "At least it's one less of them." Even I felt he had gone too far. I demanded roughly why I had been summoned. The woman's face was bathed in sweat, a white none too clean cap covered her pale hair, she shivered compulsively, and each breath seemed difficult and painful. The two women came to help her sit up, though not over-tenderly. "Why have I been summoned?" I repeated. "I, Hannah, have no one..." her breath came in short gasps "...my husband John Gill is away in the Upper Dales... Tell him... tell him... that... the fine is unpaid." ...She looked completely exhausted, then. "If it please thee, send to Felton village, I cannot..." Then the words, "Love... (she hesitated painfully) ...kin... Alice," were her last words.

One of the slatterns was already eyeing the dead woman's cloak in a calculating way.

"Did she have young children?" I asked the other one.

"Two bairns," she replied briefly, adding defiantly with emphasis, "Reverend sir."

A light of understanding struck me with sudden force. The most terrible shame overcame me, the worst and sharpest I had ever felt in my whole life... That poor dying woman was convinced her two little ones would be taken away. She feared to name them with her dying breath! That poor gentle soul!

I have heard of scourging by whips and scorpions, I have heard of being beset by demons. I truly believe that my own sufferings can only be described in that way.

...Her final message *must* be sent.

8 MOVING FORWARD

I really did not expect to be so transfixed or feel so emotional.

On a bitterly cold December day at a recent exhibition in the city's Art and Sculpture gallery, at a retrospective for the famous Hungarian sculptor Gizella Kertesz, I was deeply affected by one of her works. Much of it was based on natural forms, generally in an abstract style, with a wonderful sense of texture, but I was entirely unprepared for the impact of a far more naturalistic work from her earlier days. *Rude Awakening* is extraordinarily powerful, even shocking. There is ambiguity in the way the two bronze figures regard each other. An attractive, powerful looking man, with a very slight hint of menace seems to have made some suggestion to a much younger, delicate-looking woman, still a young girl, who is half drawn to him and half repelled. You can see his sense of entitlement in his gesture as he seems to reach out to her and you see her shrinking, half afraid of the situation, by her suppliant hand as she partly turns her head away. He is wearing a rather smart outfit while her clothing is virtually transparent, emphasising her vulnerability. I stared at this for a long time as the situation had a personal resonance for me. It had coloured a significant part of my life.

Eager to find out more about Gizella, I picked up a small leaflet with some biographical detail, scanning it hastily. As a very promising young actress at the Hungarian National Theatre, then under the direction of some celebrated producer whose name meant nothing to me, Gizella seemed set on a particular path. *A sudden change of direction saw Gizella Kertesz enrol at the Budapest College of Art where she started to work in stone, wood and metal. Her gifts in this field, over time, became readily apparent and were crowned later in life by the award of a special international prize in Poland.* Was there a clue in her sculpture *Rude Awakening* about this abrupt change? I was virtually certain of it, though the text here was carefully phrased: *It was not known if* Rude Awakening *had some basis in her own life, though, perhaps significantly, it was rarely exhibited – at the Sculptor's own request.*

Adrian Hazlehurst sized up his first-year tutorial group, leaving them in no doubt about the amount of work expected of them, though emphasising that he was always there for anyone with genuine difficulties. He enjoyed giving them a taster, such as John Donne's *The Good Morrow*, and asking some probing questions. English literature seemed always to attract more young females than males so there was no shortage in finding the type of young woman he was particularly interested in. There was always some mousey type, lacking in confidence who could profit from some occasional extra coaching, but he first liked to get to know his group even better. "Dig that velvet jacket!" was a muttered admiring comment, he overheard, from one of the year group of '63.

He knew exactly when to make his move and enjoyed seeing the chosen one's flattered amazement at being singled out by someone who made unsophisticated hearts beat faster. Someone with a reputation as a charismatic lecturer, good looking too, he must confess, who had not only considerable status in the university, but was also a well-known personality in the town. "A tower of strength, that chap," and "He's really putting our town on the map," were the approving phrases from some locals about his efforts to drive forward plans for a prestigious local arts centre and other regeneration projects. Others were far less enthusiastic, claiming, "Hazlehurst - he's always got to be Number One!" or "That type just has to hog the limelight!" Although he enjoyed teaching and lecturing, best of all was the adrenalin created by the sense of power. Divorced a few years ago, he saw himself as footloose and fancy-free, not that marriage had really made that much difference if he was honest.

MOVING FORWARD

There was a real thrill in picking the right student, her dazed disbelief, her sweet shyness…

Once he had gained her trust and confidence, he might subtly suggest a more flattering hairstyle or dressing in more attractive colours. He would indicate warm approval if any efforts were made. But he would concentrate mainly on tackling particular essay topics and on improving her written style. All this would usually be gratefully received. His personal study room was in a new Arts block with modern furniture – open bookcases in light wood, a no-nonsense desk with a business-like chair, and a comfortable sofa with one or two framed posters on the walls and some upright chairs for students – all not too intimidating.

As his strategy proceeded, he knew how to make approaches so gently, so unobtrusively that the young student was hardly aware of his nearness. It was all done so plausibly. As time went on, a slight confusion in her face, a timid withdrawal, then he knew he could soon begin to insinuate that they had a special relationship. He sensed that she longed and feared at the same time for something that she couldn't name even to herself.

It never failed. The fish would practically land itself in his net. But he knew what strings to pull if his fish refused to bite after all. Then he would whisper that it was such a pity and sigh heavily. Asked somewhat tremblingly by the unnerved young girl to explain. Reluctantly, he would add, that to lose the chance of really excellent grades… someone so promising. When the girl, bewildered, tried to make sense of this, he would continue. He really understood how she felt, and he felt compromised too. He longed for her, but risked his reputation, tongues might wag. Perhaps she found him too old, too hideous. A head shake was the usual reply. And though actually drawing nearer, he insisted that they must put a distance between them. The girl too late realising the trap, as he embraced her warmly and muttered to her not to worry about her grades, was usually near tears by this time. Softly he would comfort her... his excitement mounted as he started to think about it...

In the summer term, Eloise, deeply upset, practically burst into Adrian Hazelhurst's study where fortunately he was alone, obviously occupied in marking a set of papers. Her eyes were red, and he asked if she had had bad news. "Yes, as a matter of fact I have," she wailed. He looked at her with some distaste but decided to be patient. "Just sit down and tell me about it."

Eloise took a deep breath, "It concerns us, both of us!"

"What could concern both of us?" demanded Adrian.

"News I have just had. I'm pregnant!"

"I thought we had taken sufficient precautions," was the reply.

"That doesn't help me. I don't know where to go or what to do."

"I presume you don't want this child?"

"It's a terrible shock. My parents will kill me. I'll lose my university place... Perhaps we could marry..."

"My dear young woman. You don't understand the rules of the game. Marriage doesn't come into it. If you want to get rid of it, I can suggest a charity in the Midlands. They can help you with your problem. Have you seen a doctor at Student Health? How far on are you?"

"I've been to Student Health. That's how I found out. It's about ten weeks, but they won't recommend termination as they say there is no medical reason to do so."

MOVING FORWARD

"Well it has to be your decision. I happen to know what that charity I mentioned will charge. I can help with finance, but that is all."

"You don't feel responsible at all for a new life?" faltered Eloise.

"Should I? Our arrangement was very much a quid pro quo. Some excellent occasional coaching and we both enjoyed one or two little episodes or so it seemed. I suggest you make your appointment with the charity quite soon." Adrian scribbled the charity details on some paper and handed it to her. "Let me know so I can organise some time off for you. It will give you some useful exam revision time."

As Adrian returned to his marking, Eloise, shocked, got up still staring at him and left the room. "How could I have been so stupid?" she asked herself and then thought about her own family's possible reactions.

She could imagine the scene. There would be shocked, hurt comments as they digested the news. "How could you spring this on us?" this from her tearful mother, and from her disappointed father, scratching his head in puzzlement, "Is this what you went to university for?" And so it would go on. She needed to take proper control of her life and decide for herself what her next steps were. It was almost like speaking aloud.

I really can't face telling them. But they do have very serious worries too, particularly now. My timing couldn't be worse. My sister's baby boy needs a serious heart operation. Obviously, they're upset and frightened. So that's how I found myself in a minibus with a number of other women on a motorway to the Midlands, with little real memory of most of that day, except that nobody talked to each other. Afterwards I can remember going down in the lift as the anaesthetic began to wear off and

42

hearing someone moaning. When I looked round, I suddenly realised the sounds were actually coming from me.

Through sheer determination, I managed to do quite well in my First-Year exams. Though unsurprisingly, for more than two years afterwards, I shied away from any really close relationships and protected myself by being one of a friendly informal group.

I introduced myself to everybody now as Louie, deciding that changing my name from Eloise would help me to try to bury the past.

After my degree, I decided to take a course in librarianship and met my future husband Gavin around this time. I still had an uphill struggle with trust and self-worth. What helped to keep me sane at first, was writing an account of what had happened and then revising it later. In time I came to see that my experience had in fact galvanised me into organising my own life. It had forced me first to confront the person I had been, a bit like the naïve young girl in Gizella's sculpture.

Slowly, sometimes painfully, I began to move forward. I discovered, when I started to write poetry, that I could begin to focus on issues that really mattered. But I have to smile when I remember asking Gavin whom I had only known about six or seven months, if I could borrow his surname for my writing, as Louie Berringer had a better ring to it than Louie Battersby, and I wanted to get my poems published. Surprise, and then a delighted grin, was the answer as we both collapsed into helpless giggles, Gavin asking with mock solemnity and a hint of mischief, "Does that make me responsible for any of your debts? I'll jolly well have to think about it."

My two published poetry collections have since attracted quite encouraging reviews. The satirical *Down Paradise Way* was followed by *Burrs and Sticky Buds*, with the second collection praised for its 'wry humour'. I had told Gavin at a fairly early stage in our relationship about my former experiences. He realised I was still bruised, and things were difficult for me even after the passage of time.

When he first heard what had happened to me, Gavin was so enraged, that he shouted rather melodramatically, "The rotten swine must be stopped in his tracks before he wreaks further havoc! We need to point the finger!"

I calmed him down, explaining that Hazelhurst had taken up a professorship in Adelaide, and the past was the past. It must have been about a year later, when as an old alumna, I was sent a copy of my former University's newsletter, and I found a rather fulsome obituary about Professor Hazelhurst, who had died in Adelaide relatively young, from a fatal stroke.

9 HOUSEHUSBAND

I was a little flattered when this attractive woman with auburn hair approached me in a friendly way in the school yard after I had waved goodbye to Evie and Maddy, my two daughters. She stood out from the other mums with her carefully applied make-up and smart outfit while they huddled in a drab collection of scarves, shapeless garments, knitted hats and gloves against a biting wind. I'm quite good at sizing people up, but don't always respond immediately, so people think I'm a little slow on the uptake. This can be quite useful. I could see from the glances we were getting from the others, that she was envied for her glamorous looks. One of the group of women gave her a discreet 'thumbs up' and I smiled to myself. Two could play at such games.

"So, is this your regular job now?" she asked with a wide smile. I nodded, grinned and made to go.

"Are you one of those 'new men' who keep house?" she purred. "What should we they call them... househusbands, dreadful word, isn't it?" looking now deeply into my eyes as she asked her questions. Obviously, she must have seen me around previously. I had three options – a brusque put-down which I would regret, a pretence of being thrilled to be noticed, but this could be misinterpreted. Best of all, I could give a good impression of being stupidly boring.

"I do work from home," I said. "It can be very useful. When the boiler packed up the other day and we had no hot water or heating, I spent ages looking at details of replacements, ringing up repeatedly to get someone to come round. You'll never guess what was wrong with the old one... the..."

At this point she had already taken a step back. "Poor you!" she commented, looking for an escape route. "You haven't heard the best bit," I said quickly, but I must confess, I wasn't

45

sure what that was. "Must dash!" she claimed, flashing me a 100-watt smile.

"Too many chores!" I added, nodding at her sympathetically as she raised her eyebrows. Nice-looking woman, lovely hair, I thought. Looks like a full-time job to keep everything that way.

Ellen and I had made a pact years ago. If we had any children, she would do most of the child-care in their early years, but as soon as they were safely at their first school, she wanted to return full-time to the legal profession. She was prepared to go on refresher courses to make herself more employable. I worked for a publisher who specialised in literary fiction, principally as a reader, recommending and criticising, a job which I could do equally well part-time from home. I explained to my boss that phone, fax, electric typewriter and Amstrad word processor were all available at home. Forward planning meant I could still come into the office for any crucial meetings. My boss, originally astonished and not terribly enthusiastic about my proposition, eventually agreed to a trial period. Thankfully, he decided after a while that things seemed to be working out, but then said he would keep it all under review.

I also did very occasional freelance translation work from German, which kept me from getting stale from my main work. It all seemed to go quite well, though it was a challenge at times when the children were ill or at different schools for a while or even when one of them wanted to stay later for some after school activity. But things did get easier as they got older, however not entirely.

Ellen found herself increasingly with longer working days. She was keen to make progress in her profession; not that easy in the seventies and early eighties when a woman was usually seen as the homemaker, with at the most, only a part-time job. It meant she had to work even harder to prove herself. Our girls had reached their teens and there was a fair amount of testing the boundaries as you might expect. Ellen was super at sorting the girls out at that stage as she seemed to have great reserves of patience. We were both sharing the chores, but I hadn't quite bargained for Ellen bringing work home too. So, I was still doing most of the running around and balancing my publishing and translation work; the result was I felt totally jaded. Though, to be fair, the girls did help out sometimes.

Although we were devoted to them, to be honest, a helping hand with homework could seem like a step too far some days. I seriously began to have regrets about my work-life decision. But I didn't yet dare ask Ellen if she felt the same way. There must have been some really positive things in our lives, but it began to seem as if we had grown away from each other and everything became more of a daily grind. Ellen was also expected to turn up to a number of work-related social events, the occasional conference and late meetings. I needed to get to the office now and again and attend the odd publishing 'do'. I now felt I hadn't signed up for all of this. This relentless perpetual motion and acrobatic balancing act. It seemed my world had narrowed, hers had expanded.

Just when I felt at my lowest ebb, out of the blue my mother rang me to say she and Dad had bought a house in Spain near the coast with the help of an unexpected inheritance. The house needed a few repairs, but she was keen to invite all four of us to stay there in the summer. I confessed Ellen and I were desperate for some time on our own, just a few days, as we were both exhausted and needed space to talk things through. She listened carefully and said, "You both need a break as soon as possible. Just give me a day or two."

"Ellen, you look really down at the moment." Val was a really trustworthy older friend, so I decided to get things off my chest.

47

HOUSEHUSBAND

"Val, I don't know how it is, but if you're a man and you decide to work from home and look after the children, you are often seen as unmanly in some way.

"Then people start to say after a while, "Poor chap, he does ever so well. You've got to admire him!""

"There's quite a bit of truth in that," Val admitted. "So, what according to you, do they think about the woman as main breadwinner?"

"It seems if a man is in that position, the woman must be rather hard-hearted or perhaps even a bad lot and an unnatural mother. That's the common view."

"Ellen, surely that's an exaggeration! You're just over-worked, stressed. You've both shown that this can work. You've done it together for years. Think of those women who're actually on their own and have to try to juggle children, job and chores, often on a very limited budget. Don't give up now. Don't lose your chance of promotion in what I gather, is a very good firm of solicitors."

"Yes, You're right! Many women are much worse off, and I shouldn't complain. But sometimes every mishap seems to be blamed on my presumed absence as a nurturing parent. Strangers and some of our relatives feel free to criticise me for my apparent lack of maternal feeling. They can have no idea how that hurts and what the decision to work full-time really costs me. Evie and Maddy and family life – it all matters intensely to me. Yet I am ambitious, keen to make a real career out of law, not for selfish reasons. I hope to look back and feel I have perhaps helped to blaze a trail. But now the incredulity and downright spite I still encounter, still has the power to hurt."

HOUSEHUSBAND

"I have to tell you that I admire you tremendously in many ways. Gareth of course too. I would never have had the courage. You were right to be tenacious about the goal you set yourself... but feeling bitter won't really help. It's self-destructive. Perhaps you need to be a little less defensive, grow a tougher skin. Maybe you should be less on the look-out for comments and slights. Try to relax more, occasionally even admit your difficulties."

I did think over Val's comments, which were not totally welcome. Gareth has always been a real tower of strength, I never really lost sight of that. But I started to think about the person I seemed to have become. I'd lost my sense of humour, my more light-hearted, fun-loving side seemed to have vanished. We had now reached a point in our lives where I felt sure neither of was truly happy. Why these feelings now? Our two girls were in their teens, basically doing well and we were both very proud of them. Yet I felt consumed with guilt. I felt I ought to be able to show them even more how much I cared about them. Had I damaged their chances in life in some way? Would they look back later and say things like, "Mum was never really there for us." There was no way back then that we could have afforded paid help on a regular basis. Both our families lived some considerable distance away and had their own lives.

Friends and relatives used to ask me why I didn't go into teaching instead.

"You've much better hours for bringing up children," they had all assured me.

"But I don't want to teach. It's not really me," I would answer." Heads would be shaken at my obstinacy.

"Why not wait till they're older, then work full-time?" That was another question I fielded, explaining it didn't work that way.

HOUSEHUSBAND

What they didn't know was that I was often consumed with guilt. Had I sacrificed too much? Just occasionally I confess I wished I hadn't persisted with my professional goal. Was a good chance of a partnership in a solicitor's practice really worth so much? What was the real effect on Evie and Maddy? Had I ruined Gareth's career? Would he have preferred to be in full-time work or at least go back to it sooner? He seems to be contented enough with his work for his present publisher. But is he really? Has my own struggle been worthwhile? Most women would probably have settled for some kind of part-time work to help to balance the household budget.

I thought back to the lunch I had had ages ago with Aunt Edith, my mother's unmarried sister. She was a distant presence in my life, appearing occasionally out of the blue. She seemed to have moved home several times to various parts of the country. Aunt Edith was not a favourite with me, and it was probably mutual, but she felt it was her duty to see me now and then, usually at a restaurant lunch just for the two of us to tell me some home truths. When she first discovered the work-life arrangement Gareth and I had, she had stared at me speechlessly and dropped her cutlery as she was about to put a piece of steak in her mouth.

The waiter rushed forward to help her. Fortunately, we were sitting in a quiet corner of a largish restaurant. When she had recovered a little, she was forced to moderate her rather emphatic tones as some of the other diners started to look rather curiously in our direction.

"Ellen, I would never have believed that you would sacrifice your husband and children for your own whims in this way. You are damaging your relationship with all of them. I think the whole thing is quite outrageous. I am deeply upset." I told her that I was sorry she felt that way, but I felt I needed to be out in the world, contributing in a small way through my work to society. I needed to identify myself not just as a mother and wife, but as an individual.

"Poppycock!" she snorted. Then she stared at me, asking in what way leaving my children and husband to fend for themselves and not being there for them, could possibly help society. I tried to explain a little about my work and how satisfying it was, and at the same time, how much my family meant to me. She shook her head.

"You are an extremely selfish young woman and don't deserve Gareth, or the blessing of your two children."

The harangue made me close to tears and I was grateful when she said, "No I won't have a dessert. I couldn't eat another mouthful!" She told me she would be in touch with Judith, my mother, and swept out. I felt first of all really angry, then a little worried after she left. She was my aunt after all. I badly needed a coffee before I actually paid the bill. As I sipped my drink, I pondered on the scene.

What had really upset her so much? I felt I knew very little about her. I tried to think back. Wasn't there a rumour of a fiancé who had died unexpectedly? Maybe the outburst was real regret that she had lost her own chance of having children and a family? In a way, I may have misjudged her, but there was so much pent-up bitterness. I still felt pretty angry and decided to ring my mother too and tell her about my lunch.

Dad answered the phone. Mum was out at some class she goes to. I told him some details. "You are asking about Edith. Your mum always calls her 'a restless, unquiet spirit.' They're a bit chalk and cheese those two, tend to keep well apart. Edith's a bit younger of course."

"What does she mean about Edith being an 'unquiet spirit?' I queried.

HOUSEHUSBAND

"Well, a while after the war she went off, I think it was to the Hebrides and ran a post office and village shop up there for several years. Then the next thing we heard, she'd opened a cake and bread shop in the Midlands. It did rather well, in fact she opened one or two others as well. Then suddenly she sold up and went off to Canada. There was a rumour about her getting in with some acting company, helping out. I don't know if it was even true. All I know is she came back, and now has an address in Somerset, somewhere a bit remote, your Mum said. We haven't a clue what she's doing now."

"She must be a good organiser and quite adventurous, but she can be really quite vicious. That I'm afraid I can't take."

"She's a disappointed lonely woman," Dad answered thoughtfully. "I suppose she's been mourning all her life for the person she lost."

"Dad, you've made me feel a bit better just talking to you. Love you."

He chuckled, "Don't let Edith get you down. We're right behind you Ellen, whatever you and Gareth decide to do."

"Gareth, we've had an idea."

True to her promise, my Mum got back to me. She and Dad wanted to give us a special 20th wedding anniversary present; the date was only about three weeks away. The trip was on them, we just needed to sort out actual dates for our few days. They would come and look after the girls as they were both free. My dad had very recently taken early retirement.

HOUSEHUSBAND

"Mum, I don't know what to say..." but she went on, "We can't wait to see our granddaughters. We just don't see enough of them, so thanks aren't really needed."

I teased her, "I can see you're looking forward to spoiling them," and she just laughed.

"Seriously, you and Ellen need a bit of time to discuss details. Ring me as soon as you can." It was a wonderful surprise. Ellen would surely be thrilled too.

Two figures, a man and a woman, had stopped on their walk and were staring upwards. It was early February with only a light covering of snow on the ground, ice patches were gleaming like dulled steel. A captivating beauty lit up by some silvery sunlight, showed the most extraordinary sky. The topmost cloud layer was a shimmering mixture of finely watered silk, azure shading to soft whiteness. The next level of banked clouds, topped by mounds, was divided by a narrow ravine. Nearest the horizon was a vivid stream of sparkling blue. The scene was un-scrolling like the parting of misty curtains for some dramatic debut. Down below shapes of low-lying hills, brightened by snow, emphasised every feature, with fields penned in by drystone bulwarks. Further on were lynchets, older terrace-style field strips, etched into the hillside. On the ground an intricate stencilled pattern of boot and pawprints had left their marks on the route.

"I wish we could climb up there to those amazing skies!" Ellen said smiling mischievously. "We'll need to talk about it properly," Gareth replied, grinning, moving even closer and clasping her warmly. "But it might just be worth it!"

10 CAROLINE MENSTONE

A strange thing happened to me at the museum where I usually work in the Archives department. As a professional archivist I am normally very meticulous in what I do, everything is carefully planned, recorded and listed. Though I do have a more private, creative side, when I enjoy writing short stories and even poetry, published under a pseudonym, to avoid any possible conflict with my employers.

A few weeks ago, I decided to look for a certain eighteenth century will, which could be useful material for part of a display we hoped to mount in our museum later in the year. I found the will in an inner sanctum in the basement, but my eye was then caught by an old museum-issue cardboard box from the 1950s, with a label saying "1770s-1780s" followed by a question mark. Inside the box was a book in beautifully tooled leather, which could originally have been blue and had now faded to light grey, with some decorative half-faded gilt scrolls and what looked like a silhouette of a lady's head in neo-classical style. All my instincts said Georgian period. I sat down to read the contents with great interest, all written in slightly sloping yet firm handwriting. It became clear that this book with few dates, was not so much a diary as a book of jottings, memories and private thoughts, written by a highly successful Georgian entrepreneur, who was a woman. This was certainly unusual and a great find. I left one or two loose documents in the box for later as well as some object wrapped in a piece of cloth which looked intriguing.

The book would have to be photographed, measurements taken, weighed, the paper quality assessed, checked for any watermarks, taken for further tests to assess more clearly the paper source, its binding and so on. The handwriting would be analysed, references in the text followed up, records checked for genealogy, the style in which the book was written examined and much more. It would all take many months or longer as there were of course more urgent priorities. I would set the usual initial processes in place, fill in the necessary paperwork and make a report to my line manager at the museum. But my first step would be the Acquisitions Register to see who had brought the box with its contents into the museum and when. We then might be able to trace back some other interesting information. A quick computer check revealed that a more recent entry listed the box and its contents as probably belonging to the Georgian period, though it stated that many of the museum's earlier records had disappeared in a fire in 1940. (Perhaps it was a result of the Blitz bombing raids as we were near enough to London.)

I found myself getting very absorbed in the potential details of my Georgian lady's personality. There might be references in other diaries of the period or in a variety of other documents if she was well-known in some capacity. All this careful investigation would take considerable time. Perhaps I would have more chance to do this at a future date. But after some thought, I decided I might write my own version of her story, deliberately giving my heroine a different name and changing some details; a way of giving myself complete freedom to write and maybe even publish my fictional version.

But first I had to return to my day-job and spend time on the computer, commenting on a recent policy document which needed my undivided attention.

A few days later, I was able to return for a short space of time in my lunch break to my interesting lady. Here are my initial thoughts and findings.

Caroline Menstone, the name I have given her, seems to have bought and owned a factory for making a variety of artificial stone which seemed to be used for garden ornaments and statues as well as for the frontages of some buildings. I had already discovered this from an early entry.

CAROLINE MENSTONE

"I listened very attentively to John Hardaker for some time, as he detailed the various aspects of the stone manufactory I had bought. I noted carefully many salient points. After some further discourse. I desired that he would inform the workers that the new owner, Mrs Menstone, wished to speak with them. Then she would allow herself to be conducted round her new premises. (It now behoved me to view the workers at their tasks for an initial judgement to be formed.)"

One loose paper in the box appeared to be a battered-looking invoice or delivery note of the period and the date appeared to be 1771 for what appeared to be some stone chippings. It was made out to Mrs Menstone, but other details were either missing or so far not very legible. This date could be a possible starting date or might even give the year of her purchase of the Works. Though she might of course have bought the place even sooner. At some early stage, it seems, she changed the name of the factory and gave it her own name – Menstone – so that there was no doubt about who owned the premises and who was in control.

On a later occasion I noticed a letter carefully slotted into the book so that both sides of it could be read as I leafed through the volume.

The Limes, in the year of our Lord september 1785

To my dear Niece Caroline!

My dear, you will forgive an old man in indifferent health for a correspondence which is somewhat less punctilious than usual. I take the warmest interest in anything that affects you and I have watched your career with great interest and much admiration. Your honoured father, who was also my brother, God rest his soul, found himself once or twice in straitened circumstances – a matter of, sadly, some unwise business decisions. Forgive me, my dear, if this pains you. I do not intend to do so. I came to my brother's aid on the first occasion but regret that I was unable to furnish him with better means on the second, having my own difficulties at the time. You yourself became the family's saviour, by taking on a retail drapery your father had received in lieu of payment and turning it into a highly profitable business – a place that he saw initially as a millstone. You showed great qualities, my dear, and a formidable head for business and organisation.

Nonetheless I was taken by surprise, when some years later you decided to put this business up for sale and take on an ailing manufactory, which specialised in the production of artificial stone. I remember I did offer some advice at the time about the risks of such an undertaking, but you furnished me with some cogent reasons and have confounded any critics; nay I suspect, you have surpassed even your own most sanguine expectations.

My dear Caroline, I fear that maybe vigour and energy may wane somewhat with the passing years. On occasion it is good to breathe purer air and take more respite. Humour me by giving due consideration to the proposal I wish to set before you. It has been my pleasure to receive you at my property on the south coast, The Limes, when I was not engaged in business in London. Sadly, those occasions were infrequent. But I was able to assure myself that your eye for beauty was as keen and appreciative as your managing skills are formidable at your own manufactory. My premises are now larger than I need, assuredly so since the demise of my dear wife your aunt and my advancing years. Already I have put in hand an offer on smaller premises. Do me the honour of accepting The Limes as my gift to you. It is a place to refresh your spirit after the fogs, dust and dirt of our great capital city and would much gratify me.

Pray my dear, pardon my urging. Should you accede to my offer, you will give great contentment to an old man in the last years of his life. My lawyer already has the necessary papers to hand to progress this matter further if desired.

The house and gardens are ripe for some improvement after these many years.

Your loving uncle William.

I then turned some pages of Caroline Menstone's book and came across an exquisite drawing of The Limes, with Caroline's signature and the inscription "A wondrous gift! The Limes near Lyme Regis – my Uncle has been greatly bountiful!"

I knew from some of my own previous researches, that women with a dissenting or non-conformist background, such as Caroline, appeared to have had "a strong sense of entitlement" – they felt they had a claim to their own identity and individuality, and where possible, tried to forge a least some measure of independence. It was estimated that as many as one in five Georgian women would remain unmarried at a time. A middle-class woman without means of support and without skills, could remain dependant on her relatives and live, if unlucky, as an undervalued figure in the household. Girls and women could be left without an income of their own, or virtually so, at whim; with an eldest son inheriting the lion's share of any assets, and any younger sons next in line before the daughters. Marriage for women in Georgian England seemed to be common around the ages of 25 or 26, so that even young women who later married had to live some years as a dependant. I was to discover that Caroline's story was rather different.

She refers at one point to a letter from a much younger, recently-married friend, whose older husband appears to dog her footsteps suspiciously wherever she goes and where there is no privacy even to write a letter, unless she retires to her small, rather airless closet for her "devotions". Caroline comments rather satirically: "Such are the consolations of matrimony!" Yet though the patriarchal system reinforced marriage as the real destiny of a single woman, a wife was not always treated with the respect and status a mistress of the household might expect. My interest in Caroline Menstone steadily increased.

We find her entertaining two friends to "a dish of tea" – each of them a single woman in Georgian England, but each with a rather different experience. Caroline herself has the courtesy title of Mrs as was usual for a woman operating as an entrepreneur in Georgian England; albeit a somewhat unusual role. Miss Belinda Robbins, a virtually "portion-less" spinster, has lived unhappily in her brother's family, enduring many slights, and in no position to object to her treatment. While Mrs Selina Davenport has been a widow for many years, living formerly with a miserly husband who also had a roving eye. She has no plans to change her status and is happy to continue to be her own mistress.

These three ladies, no longer young, were sitting around a mahogany table covered with a starched white cloth and some pretty tea-things, including a silver tea kettle. All the ladies had stylish caps on their heads, though their dresses were in muted, sombre shades. They were sitting with their heads close together as they exchanged confidences, occasionally sipping their tea or crumbling a piece of seed cake. The youngest of them seemed to be in a state of some excitement: Miss Belinda Robbins looked flushed, even animated, but had slightly disarranged the fichu or dainty covering over her neck and shoulders. After the usual courtesies had been exchanged, the others waited for her to speak. "My dear friends, you will allow me the freedom to call you so?" the other two elegantly inclined their heads in assent. Miss Robbins took a deep breath, "I am out of my prison. I am like a caged bird that has to learn to fly..." The others waited, still mystified. "I have burst my bonds. I can hardly speak... But I will try to explain... I have never said much about my circumstances. We are always told that we must be grateful for what we have. That others are suffering greater pangs and our reward will be in the Hereafter... We must above all always put our trust in He who is above us who will come to our aid and reward us." "Yes!" broke in the widowed Mrs Davenport, a rather stout lady, swathed in a plum coloured gown, and wearing a truly fantastic beribboned confection on her head, "Perhaps my dear, our patience is being stretched here just a little with your sermon," she added in rather vinegary tones. Miss Robbins who was a diffident soul, opened her mouth to speak and shut it again, looking appealingly at Caroline Menstone. That lady resisted the temptation to rebuke her impatient friend and smiled warmly at Miss Robbins. "My dear, take your time. I hope it is good news!"

"Oh ladies, it is the best possible news for me – I have been left a fairly substantial legacy, enough to deliver me from the tyranny of my brother and his wife, not to mention their servants who take their tone from their master and mistress, slighting me without fear of retribution... I can now set myself up in lodgings as my own mistress in two or three rooms and there will be enough for some furnishings and a little maid servant." As she finally paused for breath, the other two offered their warmest congratulations and asked if she had already found her premises. It seemed another friend in lodgings had strongly recommended some vacant rooms near where she lodged in another part of the city. Miss Robbins had already viewed what had proved to be rather attractive premises and, best of all, they were within her means. As she hinted, at last her personal property would be inviolate, without attempts being made to unlock her desk and read her private papers. She would be able to invite her friends to drink a cup of coffee or tea or even chocolate – whatever pleased them. They smiled and said they would be honoured and delighted. Though Mrs Davenport tried to ascertain if the new address was in a sufficiently fashionable area, but Miss Robbins refused to be cowed. Instead she turned to Mrs Caroline Menstone and asked her advice on curtaining and bed hangings. Would moreen [a ribbed hard-wearing fabric] or glazed chintz be more suitable, remembering her friend's years in charge of a retail drapery. "I hear that yellow is quite the new colour," Miss Robbins enthused. "Perhaps yellow curtains and I believe that walls could be hung with a patterned paper which could just hint at the yellow, but still look distinguished." Both ladies were only too glad to advise, and Mrs Davenport begged her friend to take care that she did not over-burden her finances and hinted mysteriously that she should try to avoid entanglements.

Caroline Menstone at once saw that, though the widow had meant well, her lack of delicacy was too much for her younger friend. She decided to make some useful suggestions, offering to introduce her to one or two reliable emporiums, once Miss Robbins had time to consider her needs. Her friend responded with gratitude. As the two ladies took their leave of their hostess, Caroline's elegant dress caught their eye; their friend certainly had presence and some style – indeed, her newest lodgings with its furnishings suggested a genteel prosperity. A burst of low-lying sunlight suddenly brightened the room, dwelling on some brass firedogs and a mirror in a silver frame, before hovering over Miss Robbins' delicate features.

On yet another occasion I could not resist looking towards the end of Caroline's book, presumably written in the later stages of her life, and saw what I can only describe as a sort of personal balance sheet, which I will try to summarise. Caroline is always careful not to be thought too vainglorious and is at pains to stress that the "skills of others besides her own diligence" had made some contribution. She sees herself as an extremely fortunate person.

Her positives are that she has made an ailing business into an unqualified success. Part of that success was achieved by her own help and encouragement in improving the formula for the artificial stone, she named Menstone, and by her undoubted talent for management. She is ahead of her time by deciding to advertise in suitable journals. I then remembered I had seen something that looked like an early advertisement in one of the loose sheets in the box. This rather tattered sheet of paper was headed by a large drawing of a stone lion, with the strapline, *Menstone Artificial Stone for Strength and Durability*, followed by the address of the Works itself, too battered to read easily. Caroline seems also to have built up a network of contacts to help promote her work by word of mouth. Menstone artificial stone was praised by her clients as I found from later hints, as extremely long-lasting (so the claim in her early advertisement was not excessive) and was also seen as easy to use. Architects and interior and landscape designers (with some very famous names here which she leaves only as coded references), were all apparently happy to make use of Menstone artificial stone. As she herself states, she had earned "respect and status," and also shown that a woman could take the helm and achieve notable things as an entrepreneur in what was very much a man's world.

It is probably Caroline's non-conformist background that makes her take earnest stock of her life. Yet she does not just ask herself what success has brought her, and interestingly, does not mention material things. But she also questions if there is anything she has lost by focusing her life so much on her business. She never married or had children, though there are one or two hints of offers of marriage or potential offers. She was shrewd enough to be wary of fortune hunters as her "Works" became increasingly known. She says firmly, "I decided liking was not enough." She makes it clear that she was not prepared to give up her work "and take instruction from a husband, simply because he was a husband." She knew that she would lose her financial independence if she married. The law then was that a wife's fortune or former earnings, if any, and her person would become her husband's property on marriage. Her duty would be the running of the household and the care of any children a couple might have. It would take as late as 1882 with the Married Woman's Property Act, before there were really significant changes in the law for married women. For Caroline Menstone it is clear, that to be her own mistress was something essential for her self-worth.

I have tried to live my life according to the Scriptures, making the most of such talents as I have... Some of my sketches and designs that have occupied my leisure time and given me enjoyment have, from time to time, also been used for my business interests... I do not regret this. My only real regret is that there is no direct family member to inherit the Menstone works when I wish to retire. Though a more distant relative on my mother's side, a cousin-german, George Ogilvy, has shown some interest. My hope is he will take on the family name should he decide to take on the Menstone Works. It would mean much to me.

There was certainly one moment much earlier in the firm's history when a near catastrophe was narrowly averted. Returning to her Works after a minor purchase in the area, Caroline met a young architect and designer who had already used her artificial stone on several occasions. She remembered admiring some of the beautiful moulds Mr D- had designed for the salon of Lord M-. Mr D- had recently been away for some months travelling in Italy, financed by one of his aristocratic clients. She asked with some civility about his travels. His eyes shone as he started to mention some of the great paintings, sculptures and buildings he had seen in Rome and Venice while she smiled encouragement. As she was about to take her leave, he begged her pardon in advance and hoped that she would not think him too forward, and allow him to indicate something which was probably a misunderstanding. Permission was granted, as she told him, she could be found in her room at the Works between certain hours. At that, seeing he still looked rather constrained, she asked for some indication as regarded the "misunderstanding". He related that coming to the Works after his Italian trip, to settle an outstanding account, he was told by one of the workmen that Mrs Menstone "was gone away". However, Mr Hardaker received him with great politeness, dealt speedily with the transaction and copied the details into a ledger. But when he examined the receipted account more carefully at his own premises, the name Mrs Caroline Menstone had been crossed through as proprietor and the name Mr John Hardaker was hand printed in neat letters instead. He remembered that as he was leaving, Mr Hardaker had made a remark about the constant burden on time for a proprietor like himself. Mr D- regretted he did not have the recent document on his person. But he could call tomorrow afternoon with it if convenient. She thanked him, but asked that he send the document round to her lodgings that evening, indicating her address, adding the "gone away" had referred to a visit she had made to her uncle on the south coast. He thanked her and bowed a farewell. Measures, she decided, must be speedily undertaken to clear up this situation.

However, Caroline knew that the matter was potentially a very serious one and would test all her skills. She needed some time to think out the full implications and the possible outcome. On her return to the Works, John Hardaker was deep in some discussion over some technical problem with one or two of the men.

Caroline sat at her desk looking through the most recent ledger, and the pile of handwritten copies of all the incoming payments which also included copy receipts. There was indeed a copy of the payment of the account in question, unblemished by alteration and a copy receipt likewise. She sat deep in thought. She was conscious that she owed John Hardaker, the former proprietor, much, though his occasional brusque manner with her had certainly not made for an easy relationship for either of them over what was at least two years. She had been determined to understand every aspect of her business. Yet she had had so much to learn about the whole process of the making of the artificial stone: about the quantities and mixture of the various substances that were needed, the delivery systems, manpower, wages paid, grievances to be sorted out, repairs to the structure and the equipment, thoughts on the possible extension of the premises and what additional staff might be needed... the list was endless. For over two years they had both toiled till they were bone-weary – she herself responsible for the paper-work and the over-all management, John Hardaker for the more technical aspects, working almost tirelessly among the men, solving problems, chivvying those who were slacking, normally with a bluff geniality the men enjoyed, but he could emit deafening roars of rage if he felt that someone was not working hard enough or even endangering themselves and others by some foolish or dangerous activity. Though he was prone at times to make decisions on impulse, which could call his judgement into question, he certainly had earned their respect. Yet she and Hardaker generally had worked well together. In fact, once the men had finally begun to realise that their new owner was determined to improve the business and had begun to achieve results, she too began to have a rather special status in their eyes.

The initial problems when she first bought the Works, she soon discovered to be principally that John Hardaker, as the previous owner, had tried to do the paperwork himself as well as manage all other aspects of running the premises. If he now felt dissatisfied, discussions could have taken place. But seeing that things were working well, he probably regretted selling the Works, and regretted agreeing to stay on for a time too. It almost certainly looked as if she would have to replace him. Though that person would have to be someone with special qualities. Yet she was fully aware of the magnitude of the task. Perhaps it was time for other changes too. She would suggest a meeting with John Hardaker for tomorrow to try to resolve some of the issues.

CAROLINE MENSTONE

Caroline had arranged to be sitting at her desk, apparently absorbed in some paperwork as John Hardaker came into the small room principally used by her to attend to all written matters and where she used to meet her more important clients. Hardaker was looking a little overheated, with some fine dust on his clothes. He excused his appearance, and explained there were things he had needed to attend to and if she granted him a few minutes more, he would return in better order. As he re-entered, she pointed to a chair facing her desk, keeping her own seat behind it with easy access to her papers. She opened by asking his opinion about looking for a second in command under himself and also if it would be useful to employ a trustworthy youngster to do the basic copying of the accounts, and for making legible entries into the day ledger and other similar tasks. After all, business was good and they had every hope of expanding further. Hardaker seemed surprised and rather unsure of himself. Caroline also gave him to understand how much she valued his work and hoped that he too was content with what seemed to be a promising future.

At length, he burst out: "If Madam is so satisfied with my endeavours, it was not known to me." As Caroline was about to remonstrate as regards the veracity of this statement, he then declared in biting tones, "Some might have thought of the word partnership by now." Caroline confessed that that word had not crossed her mind, nor was it likely to.

John, now red in the face, retorted, "Of course Madam, I forgot, class is an issue here. Though I do beg your pardon," he added in a perfunctory tone.

Caroline mastering her own anger at this rudeness, handed him the receipted account she had received as requested from the young architect and asked him for an explanation of the alteration. "There is no problem about your signature on the receipt which was perfectly proper. However, for whatever reason, my name on the account as the owner has been crossed through and the name Mr John Hardaker neatly hand printed underneath, Furthermore, I understand that on that particular occasion, it is believed that you claimed verbally to be the proprietor of these premises."

Hardaker stood up, leaning over the desk, "That young whipper-snapper! It was in sport! Both what I said then and what I wrote down." He then stepped back and re-seated himself with a grunted apology for this last display.

"*That young whipper-snapper*, as you call him, already has quite a reputation for his architectural and landscape designs. Since Mr D- was told first by one of our people on the premises that Mrs Menstone "was gone away", when I was actually visiting my uncle who was in poor health, and then was confronted by what looked like a change of ownership – it caused some confusion. Such rumours will seriously damage our business. It is a very grave matter. There may have been other similar occasions which occurred with other clients in my absence."

Hardaker stood up again and took one or two steps nearer the door, "Madam, you have gone too far, questioning me like this. Why would my ownership damage what was *my* own business? It is *my* formula which has made the artificial stone such a success!"

"I don't dispute that in the slightest Mr Hardaker, though I must remind you that neither was my own contribution entirely negligible as regards helping to improve the formula and especially in running the business."

"Madam, I cannot match you for hard words, my schooling is at fault. It would be better we part company for we shall not agree."

CAROLINE MENSTONE

"Sir! I believe in your agitation you forgot yourself and I am heartily sorry for it... I will expect some notice from you in writing – to allow me a little time to find a replacement... I will calculate any outstanding remuneration which will include a month from today in spite of our current differences."

As later entries proved, Caroline rose to the challenge of losing her right-hand man, and over time the Menstone works swept on to even greater success.

At last I finally unwrapped the article still left in the box, from its fine cloth – it was an exquisitely modelled mould for a female head, very much like the neo-classical lady on the cover of her book. On the back of the mould was the name: Caroline Menstone fecit and a date.

Undoubtedly! A remarkable and formidable woman!

11 SIXPENCE

"I wouldn't give you sixpence for it in old money," said the elderly man staring at what he called "a heap of upended *wooden* blocks" in the art gallery.

"I think they're actually iron, according to the label," said Ginevra mildly. "It's a bit like a human figure."

"Complete rubbish! A waste of money!" snapped the man, before stumping off to another part of the complex.

Ginevra breathed a sigh of relief. That faceless figure built of iron blocks seemed curiously soothing. There was no expression on its face, it was not judgemental. Its short arms were not poised in any threatening way. It just stood there calmly waiting. There was just a suggestion that, in spite of its weight or maybe because of its weight, it might just possibly collapse. A bit how I feel, she thought. I am standing on my very own blocks: a nice house, our son Jason enjoying his first year at uni. Tim my long-term partner on his lecture tour, absorbing all sorts of new experiences in the Antipodes. Yet the real me is grappling to stay upright on my blocks without toppling over. Sometimes I feel someone else is pulling my strings; but it least it means I don't have to think. She shook her head at her fantasy and moved on to other exhibits.

The Drinks Party was in full swing for a clutch of senior common room academics and their guests as noise levels reached a crescendo, while gossip on various university matters washed over them all like a tidal wave. In a brief lull, glamorous Eva who was lusted after by several dons, made herself heard.

"Oh! poor you, or should it be congratulations," she cooed to Ginevra. "You've managed to put our dull little university on the map, though maybe for the wrong reasons." Here she paused, knowing she had most people's attention. She smiled dazzlingly at Ginevra who did her best to smile back enigmatically.

"What do you mean?" chorused some of the voices behind her. "Come on, spill!"

"Oh! it's quite simple. Ginevra, our award-winning poet and author, has somehow got the tabloids in a twist. Our dear esteemed colleague was asked to write a review of another poet's work for some well-known literary magazine."

"So what! said a voice. "I suppose you mean Literature Now. It's what several of us do!"

"Well, apparently she trashed this chap's work. He's been rather successful with his first volume of poetry and Ginevra suggested some of the new work wasn't quite so top notch."

"Well, that's a literary critic's job," said Ruth, who was quite a friend, looking sympathetic.

"Ah, but apparently she also made some antisemitic comments in the article too, I understand," said Eva looking delighted to be the centre of attention.

"Bollocks!" said Aaron robustly. "That's not Ginny's style. She's a straight guy."

I could only stand my ground till Eva had quite finished. "I gather," said Eva now sinking her voice as she caught sight of the vice-chancellor in deep conversation with a guest. "Jerry, the vice, was furious when the tabloids approached him for comments. He said it was publicity he could do without. But that's all I know."

SIXPENCE

Here she looked at me. I stared hard at her, then looked at the circle of faces, some puzzled, others questioning, one or two accusing, and decided it was time to go home. I already had had the press hounding me as well and so had the magazine's publisher. I was very unlikely to get any more work in that quarter. Now I couldn't take any more.

Of course, as a poet and author with a decent reputation, I was called on occasionally to review some recent poetry or even the odd novel. But it was never my style to "trash" anybody, let alone make any antisemitic remarks. I had written the piece some time ago and pointed out to my editor, that this second volume of poetry was a bit disappointing compared with the poet's previous work. He had also put in a number of what I believed to be lesser known references to earlier Jewish history, without any footnotes, so it made it difficult for perhaps some of his readers to judge two or three of his poems effectively. My editor agreed with me and I thought that was the end of the matter. I know he would have challenged me if he had thought otherwise. But let's face it, if you put your work out there in print for a critical evaluation, it's a sort of compliment if someone thinks you're worth criticising. But that was not the end of the matter.

I started to receive a series of social media posts which began to increase in viciousness. I consulted my editor who thought if I didn't respond, there would be no further ammunition. I assumed the messages were from the poet himself. The first one was relatively innocuous, and I can well understand an author feeling his work was not really valued or even understood. So, I checked through my review again carefully. The smear of antisemitism was totally ridiculous. Of course, there was increasing sensitivity on this subject and I began to worry if I should have omitted such a reference altogether. My comment had been made with tact. It would have been censorship if I had omitted it. Besides I wanted people to read and understand this poet's work. Far from trashing, I had wanted to encourage him as a writer and for him to continue producing interesting work in the future.

Other problems had arisen in my own department too. I had taken some trouble to put together a future series of lectures on cross cultural literary matters with the help of some foreign language departments. The students had shown great enthusiasm and already had put their names on a list for this course. Now the prof who headed my department told me that, as a cost-cutting exercise, the lectures had suddenly been put on ice. I thought of the large amount of time I had spent trying to set this up and the difficulties I had overcome. I was bitterly disappointed.

When Tim phoned me, he bubbled with enthusiasm over the interesting time he was having and the people he was meeting. It made me feel duller than ever. But I also had the strange feeling that there was something he wasn't telling me... I couldn't really discuss my problems long distance with him or worry him too much.

As time went on, my moods increasingly began to darken. There was this feeling of bone weariness, dragging myself out of bed, and more and more that sense of going through the motions. Perhaps I had turned into one of those block figures I had seen some time ago in the art gallery. I had already closed my social media account as those poisonous messages had continued. But even if I had gone to the police, what then? The damage had already been done. Yes, I had some friends, but they weren't the sort to confide in – just fun to meet and chat with every now and again or to go to a film with. My self-esteem, or rather my confidence bruises too easily, I recognise that. I knew that this downward spiral was deeply unsettling.

I had refused to see a specialist after I had consulted my own doctor at one point about my stress problems. He talked about waiting lists and making use of the private sector for specialist

SIXPENCE

help. I was frightened, badly frightened and thought of a dark abyss, even of losing my mind. Yet for some reason I kept thinking of the scarlet creeper on the trellis in my garden, so bold so dramatic and vibrant – it was the one thing that lifted my spirits. I looked at it for ages and realised then how rapidly the year was going.

I did take on board some of the doctor's advice. "Take a walk or two to clear your head. It's best thing!"

I duly went down to the river one day to the spot where a heron often stands patiently poised, waiting to grab his fish. Today he wasn't there, just some mallards, submerging themselves and shooting upwards in great flurries of enjoyment. I walked on, sniffing the air, revelling in the freshness. Then on I went to where the river deepened and it was beautifully quiet, so restful, with hardly anyone about. I could hear the water gurgling encouragingly so I wandered further to where it started to boil over larger rocks and where there were deeper pools. I stared fascinated. Why not enter the river and immerse myself in the water, in a sort of baptism? It seemed quite a pleasing thought. I thought how calming it would all be... I longed for comfort.

A woman's body weighted with stones and oddly, an old-fashioned sixpence in her pocket, was found in the water a few hours later.

12 GOLDEN COUPLE

The insistent train rhythm finally jerked him awake and the sticky summer heat seemed to bore through the windows. Travelling back to Leeds with his wife Jenny and the twins, after their Devon holiday, Michael spotted a folded newspaper under his seat with some large headlines. The children were absorbed in a quiet game with their mother and as he looked fondly at one dark and one fair head, he realised he must have dozed off. Such a vivid dream about his old childhood playmate, Sylvia, as she raced away from him in some flower-filled park, but then turned and waved encouragement. Jenny smiled as she saw him rub his eyes and mouthed, "Make the most of it," and he nodded in agreement. He was more tired than he realised. The constant high spirits of youngsters aged six to nine – his own and his young nephews – well, what could you expect? Idly he glanced at the paper, with yesterday's date on it, August 23 1983: FUNERAL! POPULAR FORMER NEWSREADER AND WELL-KNOWN FEMINIST CAMPAIGNER! and in smaller type: *Accident Investigation...*

At first, he felt a prickle of unease, then a real shock of horror when he recognised the inset photo of Sylvia Sullivan's well-known face. No news or newspapers had reached them while they were at their rather isolated rented cottage with four lively children. Soon he would be back teaching physics at the grammar school – not bad for a lad from a secondary modern, transferred to his local grammar school at fourteen and on to a redbrick university. Sylvia! How strange to dream about her after all this time! Their mothers had been good friends long ago in Leeds and had kept in sporadic contact even after her parents moved to London. Sylvia had been the leader in their early adventures. He still remembered the thrill of exploring an old derelict building – strictly forbidden of course. There was a steep climb up the longish flight of stone outer stairs and then a dare to go into a room with blown out windows. Really creepy! Sam said a gas leak had caused all that mess. There had been a narrow door at ground level which was jammed. Martin, it would be Martin, suggested it was a 'bog'. They all giggled and screeched in delight, even more when Sandra said primly, "You mustn't use that word!"

Sylvia had found a longish wooden pole among the rubble and announced she would first test the upstairs floor with it. (The thought of his own two children trying such an escapade, with perhaps falling masonry, never mind treacherous floorboards, made him shudder.)

Martin's cheeky grinning face had pushed past to the top first, closely followed by the more serious-minded Sam. The other girl, Sandra, sat on the steps before she went in, while he himself and little David climbed up last. Poor little David, only six and dead before his seventh birthday. Some sort of fever they said – but when he was older, his mother explained it had been meningitis. What had happened to all the others? He started thinking. A passion for horses had led Sam to Ireland and on to a management role in a racing and livery stable. Sandra, a Woolworth Saturday girl, became branch manageress of a medium-sized store near Manchester. Martin first joined the entertainment staff at Butlins holiday camps in Skegness, then in Paignton. But to everyone 's astonishment, he found his true niche in his uncle's insurance firm in Leeds where he was doing rather well... But Sylvia was the real star.

"Sylvia!... Craig! How divine you both look, darlings!" Faces turned from a striking vision in an artfully draped moss green gown, with bracelets decorating rather beautiful arms, and an exotic gold cap on her head, as she smiled and made dramatic welcoming gestures to the handsome couple who had just entered the art gallery, where the launch of some contemporary artists' works was taking place.

75

GOLDEN COUPLE

There was a real buzz as the couple walked forward. Remarks were heard on all sides. "Who's the girl in green, anyway?" was first demanded.

"That's Elfrida MacGregor, always adds a bit of drama to a glittering throng."

"But who's the other one with that chic hairstyle and stylish white dress with floating sleeves, she's really beautiful!"

"It's a dream that dress – gorgeous jewelled neckline. Looks like real turquoises, could be pearls too and silver lozenges!"

"I've just recognised her, it's Sylvia Sullivan, you know, the television newsreader."

"That good looking chap? Oh, he's her husband, Craig Arbuthnot – Arbuthnot Sports Enterprises Ltd."

"Lucky girl, he's made millions, or so they say."

"She's really lovely – doesn't need all that make-up they make them wear on the box."

Elfrida was now ushering the couple towards a rather tall young man with crisply curling hair, who was looking slightly amused at the proceedings.

He was introduced as Gilles Hendrickx, Elfrida's Belgian cousin, who was spending a few days in the capital. Greetings were exchanged, with Craig now waylaid by a couple of businessmen he knew slightly, who insistently demanded Craig's opinion on the state of the markets. Craig responded with knowledgeable charm. "What do you think, Craig, about investing in one or two of those paintings here?" quizzed the stouter of the two men, taking out an elegant leather-bound notebook.

GOLDEN COUPLE

"I'd be interested to have a look, but have absolutely no expertise in these matters," Craig assured them. "Then making a graceful excuse to the other three, Craig was led away, with the other man enthusing, "Give me textile patterns – sludgy colours – just the thing for the drawing room."

"Are you impressed by any of the paintings?" Sylvia asked Gilles. He smiled and gave a slight shrug. "I came with Elfrida, who enjoys looking at art. Though I did like the one with the birch trees standing round a small dark pool – a nice effect of light."

Before Sylvia could respond properly, Elfrida cut in, "Now you two, I forbid you to talk French to each other," and as the other two stared in surprise.

"Sylvia studied French at the Sorbonne in Paris you know. But I won't understand a single word." Elfrida then became even more vivacious. She had already enjoyed a few glasses of some rather good champagne which had been handed round with the canapés and decided to give Gilles even more information.

"Sylvia doesn't just read news reports, she presents all sorts of other programmes as well - really intelligent ones." Both the others looked embarrassed at this turn of phrase.

"I specialise in aspects of European law. With an English mother and a Belgian father, it seemed a good solution," offered Gilles with a twinkle in his eye. But Elfrida, eternally restless, felt that she needed to be confidential.

"Of course, Craig spends lots of time travelling around to all sorts of countries looking after his business interests. Wouldn't stand for it myself, I'd take a lover, just to spite him."

Sylvia seemed to be taking a great interest in the elegant shoes she was wearing and finally said, patting her friend gently on the shoulder, "Elfrida you have to remember, Craig does a fair amount of trouble-shooting in his work so there are often no set hours. I too can have quite a tricky schedule – radio and television work, not to mention sudden programme changes and lots of preparation. We both knew it wouldn't be easy."

At this point, mercifully, a press photographer asked if he could take a photo of the two charming ladies who obliged, though the photographer was careful to manoeuvre both of them into suitable positions first, curbing Elfrida's attempted excesses with a practised hand. Various friends and acquaintances now swooped on Sylvia, begging for her opinion on some controversial painting at the far end of the gallery. "Do you think the artist really meant something symbolic or actually something, well phallic, really?" asked one of her friends, her eyes round with mischief and mock horror. Sylvia *must* go with them immediately and inspect it.

Michael now started skimming through some of the details about Sylvia's life in the newspaper. It was an expanded version of a previous obituary article. Sylvia had gone to a grammar school near London, studied French and Italian at Queen Mary's, London, with an additional year at the Sorbonne in Paris. It was no surprise that she got a job first at BBC Radio, then at BBC Television where she spent some time learning her trade. Her attractive voice and appearance helped to make her into a well-known presenter on various programmes and finally into a popular news reader. It mentioned she was on the panel for a late-night arts programme once and had enjoyed the experience. She also successfully co-presented a popular programme on the city of Paris. It was the period where you saw more programmes in colour, Michael remembered. There had been a high-profile marriage to a very glamorous entrepreneur, Craig Arbuthnot, whose retail sports equipment empire, Arbuthnot Sports Enterprises Ltd, stretched from the

GOLDEN COUPLE

UK to parts of Europe and the United States. The firm's logo was well-known, consisting of four different sports' balls with the initials ASE. A fairy tale wedding in 1969 was attended by famous pop stars and even minor royalty. Sadly, after two late-term miscarriages, the couple were content to remain childless. With Craig often away on business trips and Sylvia's broadcasting commitments, it was difficult for them to spend much time together.

Increasingly as Sylvia had begun to interest herself in women's rights, and realising that there might be conflict with her neutrality as regards her work for both Corporations, she decided to resign her post and campaign in areas where she felt women still had unequal opportunities, in spite of some recent legislation. Equal pay and child-care were some of her concerns, and more controversially, rape and abortion. She was to become a highly practised speaker at key conferences on women's matters and a writer of stimulating articles. She was specially invited to present some of her views as a panellist on radio. Sylvia became a tireless campaigner for her causes and was on her way to speak at a prestigious international women's conference in Frankfurt when her plane got into serious difficulties. It was not yet certain what caused the fatal crash... and great loss of life...

Craig Arbuthnot had flown back from the States for his wife's funeral and her elder sister, Claire Beaumont, who lived in Lincoln, had also attended with her family. In recent years, the Arbuthnots had still been prominent figures in the social calendar, taking in Ascot, Chelsea Flower Show and opera first nights whenever their schedules allowed, also hosting some high-profile dinners.

Michael put down the newspaper. Sylvia had been only 42 when she died. He had secretly always regarded her as way above him in the firmament. She had been about two years his senior, though she had always treated him as a younger favoured cousin. His hands shook as he put down the newspaper. He felt deeply upset at the waste of so much promise and so much vitality. But at the same time, it brought home to him with renewed force his own good fortune. He turned to his family, blowing Jenny a kiss and started to joke with the twins, Hughie and Evie, "Now which of you is the most rubbish at Hangman?" Of course, they shouted gleefully "Daddy is!" and insisted he play too.

In his letter of condolence to Claire, Sylvia's older sister, Michael explained he would have liked to have been at Sylvia's funeral, but unfortunately had missed the key announcement. Perhaps they could meet? He could travel down to Lincoln or they could meet in London if convenient, though he realised she had hardly known him. Claire wrote back acknowledging his letter, writing, "It would be a great relief to talk to someone who has warm memories of Sylvia in earlier days." At their meeting she mentioned the huge row that erupted when Sylvia told her husband she was leaving the Corporation and why.

Craig stared at his wife in disbelief. "Let me get this straight. You've decided to leave the job you loved and worked so hard for, just at the point when you've quite a decent profile in the organisation. I'll remind you too, that you chose to work. You didn't need to."

"My profile isn't that good, not where it really matters. Yes, I read the news from time to time, but these are the comments from my bosses. 'Don't distract the viewers by looking too pretty. And remember the News is serious stuff. A man really does give it more weight.'"

"But you've proved them wrong!" Craig was baffled. "You've also co-presented that programme in Paris – that went really well."

"Yes, but when I hoped for a series, I was told there was no budget."

"Come on, there was that late-night arts programme – you enjoyed doing that."

"I was only there as a token woman when lots of people were down with flu."

"But why leave? The public love you."

"I want to do other things now, not worry about my hair and make-up being immaculate and always dressing appropriately or what is considered appropriate... I don't think you have any idea of what it's like – you have to be at least twice as good at your job to be allowed some time in the sun."

Craig shook his head in exasperation, "We all have to struggle whatever the job is. It all seems a bit feeble to me. Even I must dress at times more formally than I might like. There are certain standards for business entrepreneurs too," he added with a smile.

Sylvia burst out, "It's not as petty as you think... realising that any man will be promoted above you and earn more. But it's not just the money – it's how you're valued and what opportunities you get... It's not just at the Corporation. Out in the wider world there's a lot of things wrong today with the way things are still being done. Take salaries for instance, a woman doing the same job with the same skills will be paid considerably less. It's happened with those machinists in the car industry in 1968 – that's what the strike was about, but it's only one example among hundreds and hundreds."

"Money," said Craig pointedly, "I wouldn't say we go short," he added as he looked round at their elegant lounge with its designer furniture, stylish ornaments, striking modern lamps and large windows. Outside in their gardens was an impressive modern ornamental fountain and various sculptures.

"But thousands do go short! There are other major things as well... Some women are suffering violence and abuse in their own home from their husbands, their children are terrified. They have no safe place to go to and often no money to support themselves. There was a case recently where a frightened woman called the police and begged them to come. She was being threatened by her husband with a knife. Her two young children were screaming in terror. By the time help came, she was so badly hurt that she died in hospital shortly afterwards and both children had stab wounds... How can anyone come to terms with that? There are also desperate women who need an abortion and are driven to use some unqualified back street person with catastrophic consequences. The women might have had no access to contraception in the first place or maybe their husband forbade it."

"Have you quite finished?" Craig demanded angrily with a sneer. "Right! all men are utterly revolting monsters. Or swine if you like. So, what are you going to do about it? Is this what it's all about? Which of these causes is your chosen one or is it all of them? Oh, you missed out those wretched women at Greenham Common, aren't they part of the sisterhood too? Aren't they all women's libbers?"

Sylvia furiously and cuttingly replied, "The women at Greenham Common are making a political statement, a protest against the missiles arriving at that base. I am still deciding where I can make a difference. I don't pretend to have answers, but I want to help in some way and make use of any strengths I have. I prefer to be considered as a person rather more than a smartly dressed doll with a pretty face who sometimes surprisingly actually speaks sense."

GOLDEN COUPLE

"Now I understand why you're leaving the Corporation – before they sack you – isn't there some clause in your contract – if you join some organisations, you might invalidate their famous boast of neutrality, especially if it was leaked to the press."

"As I said, I am still deciding where I can help most..."

"Good God, if you go demonstrating and camping out at Greenham Common, I can just see the headlines. You'll actually damage our own business Arbuthnot Sports Enterprises Ltd – the newspapers would have a field day *POPULAR EX-BBC NEWSREADER, SYLVIA SULLIVAN, WIFE OF ARBUTHNOT ENTERPRISES CHIEF CAMPS AT GREENHAM COMMON!*

"I'll be a laughing-stock. You couldn't have done more damage if you'd tried and thought about it for weeks... That lot seem to enjoy provoking the police, camping out in their benders, breaking into the base."

"So, it comes down to your business interests, does it? I'll really have to bear that in mind. Humanity or morality in the real sense of the word doesn't come into it of course."

"Don't give me the bleeding heart and that cant to boot. Work out how we can manage to pay for our current lifestyle, will you! Don't tell me you haven't enjoyed it! If our shares start to slide, there'll have to be damage limitation."

The phone rang and Craig rushed over to answer it, saying to his caller, "In that case I'll meet you in my office in about half an hour." Then he slammed out furiously to his car while Sylvia, totally unnerved, set off in her own vehicle in the opposite direction.

GOLDEN COUPLE

According to Claire, who was her sister's confidant, the couple had been estranged ever since that dreadful row, but somehow managed to put up a smokescreen over their relationship, to protect themselves from ever-avid press interest. Since Craig had been infrequently at their London home or even at their country 'getaway' and was known to be actively looking for various new markets in Europe and Asia, his absences were comparatively little remarked on.

Once Sylvia had left the BBC, she put out her own press statements about why she had made her decision, saying she had the highest admiration for both Corporations (Radio and Television), part of which read: *It has been a great privilege to work for these two major corporations over a number of years. Moreover, I owe a great deal to these institutions for giving me the opportunity to hone my communication skills and participate in many interesting projects.*

But for some considerable time, I have been deeply interested in specific women's issues and have tried to read extensively on such subjects, wishing to involve myself further. I now feel that the time has come when I could be of real service. I hope to contribute articles in various periodicals and participate fully in appropriate conferences without compromising the two institutions I still value so much. My decision has been very far from easy. Finally, I wish to thank very warmly the many members of the public who have been so supportive and appreciative of my work throughout many years.

Claire explained, "As Sylvia started to be offered a number of speaking engagements, she made a lot of new friends and contacts. But my sister and Craig were both shrewd and pragmatic enough to realise that there was added value for both in staying together." She explained further, that Sylvia, by carving out a new career, seemed to show Craig in a new light not solely as a business-man, but as a man who was generous enough, whether he agreed with everything his wife did and said or not, not to stand in her way, when she wished to follow causes that meant a lot to her. His clever highly attractive wife was very much seen as a business asset too. Sylvia found in her turn, in her new role as feminist campaigner, that she could still cultivate good connections with the establishment and the business world as Craig's wife. Her status seemed to confer some useful 'respectability' on her campaigning and helped her to win over the support of some very influential people."

Memorably, Claire quoted to him some of Craig's words: "It's only people who have some real feeling for each other, who know best how to hurt each other. They often leave the deepest wounds."

It seemed to Michael a most profound statement and infinitely sad. He wished he had known Craig. Two stiff-necked people!

If there hadn't been that fatal plane crash, who knows, they might have found a way back to each other... Now we would never know.

13 *NOBLESSE OBLIGE*

I, Frederick Hohenzollern King of Prussia, have graciously agreed that a royal biography be published on the occasion of my seventieth birthday celebrations. Duke Eberhard von Hohenfeld has been entrusted with this forthcoming task. It has been arranged that he will bring me some preliminary notes here today. There are some matters in my early history, which are relatively unimportant, yet a way must be found to present what is necessary. A monarch's image is paramount. There is little need to rehearse one's youthful follies.

After so many years, I find that the young man I once was has become a total stranger to me. It is well over half a century ago! I certainly no longer have anything in common with the impetuous youth who blamed himself for what he saw then as the murder of his dearest friend and tutor – Lieutenant Hans Hermann von Katte. Hans, the older by several years, must have known the risks he was taking to encourage and plan a secret scheme of escape from the militaristic Prussian court. There was the hope of finding succour in England, since my mother Queen Sophia was the daughter of the English King George I. He was then succeeded by his son George II. As a prince and a relative, I would have expected to meet with a warm welcome. I had had absolutely no thought then of any political or diplomatic consequences. The scandal if my plan had succeeded, would have been truly indescribable. I now pale at what I then contemplated. But that in no way excuses me, a young hothead, only concerned with what was happening to himself. Mercifully, our plan was discovered.

At my court martial, aged 18, I was forced to confess that I had deserted, not from battle, but in effect from the army where I had a military position, and therefore from the crown and state of Prussia. Fairly heinous crimes! I could not tell the military tribunal that my escape attempt was from the stifling and often brutal atmosphere of our Prussian military-style royal court. But I did say that I found it difficult to measure up to what was expected of me and the fault must therefore be mine. Though in my own view at the time, there were extenuating circumstances. From early childhood I had been brought up to be a soldier. But it was the verbal and physical abuse I continually suffered from my father the Soldier-King Frederick-William, which affected me. As I began to receive actual military training, I was still often physically punished and humiliated for trivial things by my martinet parent, who once insisted to me in public that my wearing gloves when out riding was totally unmanly and unsoldierly. With the wisdom of later years, I began to realise this was the way he coped with the disappointment that his son had an abiding interest in the arts, music, and intellectual matters. I also played the flute quite well, but this always had to be in secret. Above all I adored all things French, including the language – all of which our Monarch, King Frederick-William, thoroughly despised. My father was determined to remake me in his own image as a worthy successor to the Hohenzollern dynasty. With hindsight, I eventually understood his feelings much more easily.

I began to see that I had never really thought of the consequences either for myself or my poor friend Lieutenant Hans Hermann von Katte who ought to have dissuaded me from my course of action. I later realised that I had deserved to be punished, for causing Katte to desert and for the horror and dismay it would arouse for the King and court, and indeed the country. I knew my mother and sisters would sympathise with me, but they counted for very little. Worst of all, I was condemned to watch Hans' execution, which was conducted with full military ceremony. The charges were read out: high treason, dereliction of duty, plotting against the monarch and the state of Prussia, and using his position to lead the heir to the throne astray. On November 6th 1730, the drums sounded with a fearsome crash as the executioner went about his grisly task. Von Katte's white face and proud military bearing haunted me for years. All eyes turned swiftly then to me in full military uniform, appropriately wearing a black tricorne and dark jacket. I was flanked on either side by an officer, in case I should disgrace myself in some way by showing emotion. I was later told that I too might have suffered a similar fate to Hans, but the King was made aware that a Prince of the blood could only be tried by his peers. After my own court martial, I was sentenced to be imprisoned for ten weeks in the isolated castle of Kutrin, stripped of my military title, and was totally out of favour with my father. It gave me plenty of opportunity to think things out.

About a year later, the King decided on a semi-reconciliation. And a couple of years afterwards I was suddenly allowed to take part in a battle under the command of Austria's great general, Prince Eugene, who had formerly so successfully defeated the Turks and cleared Hungary of Ottoman control. Then when once again the Turks were the enemy, I saw Eugene in action as a brilliant military strategist. I will always remember the way he was able to manoeuvre his light calvary and how swiftly even the dragoons with their heavy swords and single flintlock carbines could move on the field. From then on, I began to dream about planning my own military campaigns at some date in the future.

But to return the present. I had seen Eberhard von Hohenfeld previously and instructed him to focus little on my earlier life apart from a few essential details. The emphasis should be on my later achievements and reforms where these appeared significant. He had assured me that the biography would indeed principally concentrate on my reign and the international acclaim I had received, as well as the many ways in which, and here I quote his actual words, "Prussia under his Majesty as Supreme Commander, had become a most significant player on the European stage."

At this I rose from my desk and had bowed in acknowledgment.

Today after the initial greetings had taken place, I asked how the Duke intended to deal with that difficult part of my early life.

"Your Majesty, there was no real problem. It would of course cause much talk if we omitted that youthful escapade entirely. I have explained that in your youth, you had placed great trust and even some friendship in your tutor Lieutenant Hans Hermann von Katte, who appeared to sympathise greatly with your troubles. Then for reasons of his own, he encouraged you increasingly, when your royal father was particularly enraged at your musical and intellectual pursuits, to take an extended secret visit to England. This plot was discovered, and his treason was appropriately punished by the military court with execution. You yourself had also incurred the royal displeasure and were unfortunately out of royal favour for some time."

(It was not easy to read his Majesty's rather rigid features as he then appeared to busy himself with some documents, though the atmosphere seemed to have lightened.)

"Hohenfeld, please be so good as to summarise for me those reforms and features of my reign you found especially significant. I prefer to read your account later when I am more at leisure. Though I beg of you to omit much of the more elaborate courtesies normally thought necessary, when conversing with a royal personage. My time is not infinite. It may be useful if I give you an opportunity to arrange your thoughts."

(He then turned once more to some important document, though I was aware he himself needed some of the opportunity he had given me.)

NOBLESSE OBLIGE

There are certain other areas of the King's life where I must tread carefully. I as his biographer, need to consider what to omit, especially since my subject is still alive and in charge of what is written about him. On the other hand, a biography does need some light and shade, or it becomes a list of positives without any real possibility of conveying the Monarch's character or penetrating a little below the surface. I do know King Frederick very well, but if I don't shape this biography as he likes, he will dismiss the whole scheme out of hand. His rages are well-known; he is certainly in some ways his father's son. The iron really entered his soul after that ill-thought out youthful plot with Lieutenant von Katte. Our Monarch may well be enlightened and cultured, but he is most definitely a total autocrat. Fortunately, it is not actually difficult to talk of his many successful reforms and actions. Though there are some matters in his private life where I must find the appropriate phrase or perhaps omit where necessary.

He has treated his queen, Elisabeth Christine, with great neglect and has called her "a sour-faced woman" as if she had no real personality. I believe she has had a lot to bear. Some justice must be done to her. The King believed he had done his duty by her when he begot an heir. As usual, he then went his own way. I recollect there are also rumours about the young pages and cadets at the palace of Sans Souci. It is known that some of them are treated as special favourites and can spend some time alone with his Majesty. Guests and staff at this rococo palace in Potsdam are always male.

Yet Sans Souci has become a celebrated centre where various French intellectuals gather, famed for their wit and discussions. Voltaire, the well-known writer was particularly feted there.)

"Well Hohenfeld, have you arranged your thoughts?"

(The King's glance was encouraging.)

NOBLESSE OBLIGE

"Sire, your military command and your strategy have been the envy of Europe, particularly waging war against Austria and capturing the rich industrial province of Silesia. Other military campaigns have been equally successful so that Prussia's provinces have been much extended in the north to West Prussia and your now enormously efficient army is supreme in Europe. In domestic affairs, your highness has shown great understanding, aided by your many years of private study of constitutional matters, which enabled you to reform the bureaucracy and likewise the judiciary. Your forward-thinking views on religious toleration are counted as admirable and enlightened. Your land reforms have enabled useful crops to be grown which have aided our poorer classes. And, very significantly, our present educational system is also the envy of Europe."

(The King looked impassive and seemed to wait for more.)

"As regards the Arts – at Sans Souci, your beautiful rococo palace you yourself designed, your Majesty cultivated a circle of intellectual and enlightened thinkers on various subjects, with the writer Voltaire as its apex."

(I noticed a slight flash of annoyance as I mentioned Voltaire's name, but the King knew Voltaire was a major figure. Just in time I remembered to avoid the subject of poetry. The King who spoke excellent French, had tried to write French poetry, asking Voltaire to criticise. Voltaire's caustic wit was well-known and probably exercised. There was a major quarrel, and Voltaire departed, though eventually they did correspond again.)

"As regards music, your Majesty has performed at palace concerts on the flute and even composed sonatas and concertos. Two members of the great Bach family had the honour of visiting your court as did other musicians of note."

(I stared fleetingly at the monarch with his penetrating dark eyes. He was a formidably intelligent man.)

"I see Hohenfeld, that there is perhaps an aspect of your Monarch that you have not mentioned so far. Maybe it does not seem so significant. I seem to remember that one of my first acts as King was to order the construction of the Opera House 'Unter den Linden' in Berlin."

"It was not an intentional omission your Highness. I can assure your Majesty that it is prominently featured in my draft version which you have before you. I know that music is something deeply significant for you." (There was a gracious nod and a thin smile.)

(I hoped my concluding remarks which followed, would somewhat soothe the royal nerves.)

"Your royal Highness will allow me to express the enormous pride your late father, King Frederick-William of Prussia, would have taken in your many significant achievements. Although he laid the foundation for Prussia's military exploits, you yourself, during your reign of 42 years, have surpassed many other crowned heads to become an embodiment of the Enlightenment and all its glories."

(The King responded looking first pleased and then serious.)

"I believe all this to be true Hohenfeld. I am certain my father, King Frederick-William, would see all that I have created as a real justification for his methods."

14 A FAIRYTALE

There was once a handsome king in a distant land who was a very fortunate man. He had fallen deeply in love with a very beautiful princess from a neighbouring region who loved him in return. The young people had a very happy marriage with little to vex them. The king's subjects seemed contented and their monarch looked on them with a benevolent eye, hearing their petitions and doing his utmost to maintain peace and harmony in his kingdom. A daughter was born to the couple after a few years who had much of her mother's beauty and as she grew older, her wisdom was remarked on by all who knew her. Her parents felt that they had nothing left to wish for.

However, when some time had passed, the king's trusted major-domo presented a petition from the people which stated, with many additional courtesies, that if it pleased their majesties, it might further secure the kingdom and succession should the royal couple be blessed with another infant. And should that offspring be a boy, there was perhaps less likelihood of a foreign power ruling over them. A further advantage might be that it might give the young princess, in the fulness of time, greater freedom on where she might wish to bestow her hand. The king declared that he had always seen his daughter as his true heir and fit to rule when the time came. But the major-domo assured him that his people had rather more traditional views. Besides, though the princess was in admirable health, who knew what the future held? The king, now greatly concerned, consulted his wife, remembering the difficult birth of his beloved daughter. But the queen reassured him, saying, "If heaven wills it, we will have a baby son to complete our family." Indeed, in due course, the queen was delivered of a lovely baby boy and there was great rejoicing in the land.

Yet after this birth the queen seemed to make only a slow recovery. She looked increasingly pale and tired easily, finally

93

taking to her bed. The distraught monarch sent far and wide for physicians to cure the queen's sickness, but to no avail. She became a total invalid, dying when her daughter was barely fourteen years old.

The King mourned his wife deeply and was inconsolable. But the courtiers, as time went on, began to whisper that a new wife might lessen his sorrow and cause him once more to enjoy life. Around this time too, the princess who had also loved her mother dearly, began to suffer from terrible nightmares. The court physician was prevailed upon to prepare some suitable herbal concoctions which would help the poor child to sleep more soundly. The king, her father, anxious about his daughter, would sometimes come softly into her room when she was asleep, admiring her luxurious chestnut hair and creamy complexion. It was almost as if his wife had come alive again as her younger self. The princess's graceful limbs and pink blush on her cheeks began to obsess him. He thought of her joy as she rode her favourite black mare through the forest glades, her reading and studying put aside for a time. As her father, he surely had the right to watch over her, to ensure that her sleep was not disturbed.

As he thought about her future and some bridegroom having the privilege of being close to her; it all became increasingly unbearable. Meanwhile odd rumours started to circulate at court. But the king was no fool. Gossip then began to centre on the king's various dalliances with two or three very charming ladies of the court, but there was still no sign that he might make one of them his consort.

One evening the princess woke up from sleep to find herself clutched in a close embrace. Then the person next to her rolled over and seemed to smile, murmuring her mother's name. Horrified, she recognised her father, and managed to extricate herself, wrapping herself in a warm robe over her thin nightwear and sat down in her favourite comfortable chair, deep in thought. She wished at all costs to avoid a painful scene and knew her father was a proud man.

When the figure on the bed was finally fully awake, she spoke to her father in a level tone of voice. He sat up, listening while various expressions of surprise, shame and even anger flitted over his face.

"Father, please hear me out. I have no intention of running off and hiding in the forest or being banished to some remote province," she said wryly. "However, I do not wish to make any scandalous accusations as I am aware that though I am innocent, malicious tongues could easily damage my reputation as well as yours... As a royal princess I must be above reproach."

The King started to his feet at this speech, but his daughter begged him to listen to what she had to say and to seat himself in greater comfort.

She continued, "This is what I propose. My aunt, the queen, who rules jointly with my uncle in their kingdom over the seas, has invited me as you know, to make an extended visit. There is no question that I will of course receive a warm welcome there both as your daughter and their niece. Their court is celebrated for its learning and culture. I would have the opportunity to study various interesting areas of knowledge and improve on such accomplishments as I have... It would mean a great deal to me."

The King now rose again and made to speak.

"Please just hear me out father. You owe me that courtesy... However, I do not wish to go empty-handed to my new home as if I am in disgrace. It is fitting that I go with either a dowry or a settlement, so I am not a burden to my relatives. My mode of travel, with suitable companions, should be fitting for a royal princess." In her next sentence, the princess allowed a slight tremor to become apparent in her voice. "But a visit from you and my little brother the prince, after the lapse of some time, would be really welcome."

The King stood and bowed his head in respect and admiration. "Daughter, as you are aware, I do not bow my head to anyone. But to you my daughter, who has shown wisdom and restraint beyond your years, I hope in time to earn your forgiveness for my totally unpardonable act."

15 A COMMON THREAD

I was taken by surprise, in fact completely stunned, when Adam, my live-in boyfriend, ditched me just about three weeks before my university finals. Even years later I would probably still see it as the most hurtful thing that Adam could have done and wonder about his timing.

We both had had some relationships before we met each other and had been quite open about it. I was enjoying life and my English course had had its moments. Circuit training was good fun and I had joined various clubs, including the Film Society where I had met Adam towards the end of my second year. We really seemed to click. He was a few years older, a post grad studying for a doctorate.

One evening, there was a showing of that famous early silent black and white 1920 German horror film, *The Cabinet of Dr Caligari*, with English subtitles. I decided to give it a try. The film sets were amazing, all strange angles and shapes which according to the notes we were given, were part of an art movement called Expressionism, suggesting the post-war turmoil. The film actors' make-up looked very exaggerated, but I found the story gripping all the same, with a really surprise ending. Joshua Taverner, the University's head of music, provided the atmospheric organ accompaniment.

There was a good discussion afterwards on illusion or rather delusion and reality. Adam came over, introduced himself and we started chatting, continuing over a drink. Things went on from there as we discovered we had various shared interests. He was very good-looking, with an open friendly face and easy to talk to. I caught some envious female glances at times when we later went out together. I confess I was really smitten and rather flattered as he seemed so sophisticated.

A COMMON THREAD

Then we started to meet quite regularly and before the start of my term in September, we had progressed to a shared flat. He had been working on his doctorate during the summer, some research project in which a major firm had already shown interest. I had found myself a vacation job in a big store in Liverpool as I had no real interest in returning home. A great highlight of that period for me was when Adam was given two tickets to a rather special event, a fancy-dress ball, by a business contact who couldn't use them. Adam insisted that we hire some costumes from a special shop in the city so we could really appear in style. When I worried about cost, he said it was his treat. He looked terrific in peach and cream satin as Casanova, complete with a very becoming wig. I decided to go as Cleopatra, my straight dark hair gave me the idea. The outfit was a simple white shift which skimmed my figure and some rather heavy Egyptian-style jewellery round my neck, a gilt circlet in my hair and an amazing gilt bracelet which coiled round my arm and ended in a small snake's head. Heavy eye-make up and gold sandals completed my outfit. When we entered the ballroom, there was a murmur of interest and we both felt on cloud nine. The evening became a total fairy tale. Adam whispered to me later he couldn't wait to get me back home.

However, living together was a little bit of an eye opener; lots of silly unimportant things. Adam was forever leaving kitchen cupboards and drawers open and what I really found difficult, a dirty rim in the washbasin or the bath.

Well, everyone has their foibles. I wasn't that tidy myself. I know I had some irritating habits like frequently mislaying my purse or keys, so wasted quite a bit of time with frantic dramatic searches. Then I liked to hear music while I was studying but Adam, when he was around, wasn't that keen on my choices, which were often of the classical type. When I did get some headphones, I disliked wearing them and found them awkward and heavy. In time I began to think that I was bearing most of the brunt of the shopping and cleaning, while Adam rushed out to Labour party meetings and involved himself increasingly in Student Union matters or lay stretched out on the old sofa.

A change of scene was just what we needed. This was in the shape of an invitation from Adam's parents, which turned into a very pleasant weekend in Lyndhurst, a town in the New Forest. Though Adam had warned me that his mother was often quite vague, in fact rather 'scatty' was his word and that his father was a rather hearty type, who thought a discussion was sticking obstinately to his point of view, no matter what; I found his parents very welcoming. I also enjoyed exploring parts of the New Forest, and the Lewis Carroll connection, when we found Alice Liddells's grave in an old churchyard. I also thoroughly appreciated the relaxed atmosphere of his parents' home, and rather revelled in his mother's excellent home cooking as she served up a succulent Sunday roast with vegetables and a delicious lemon meringue pie. I worried about having to invite Adam back to my father's house as Dad and I were no longer very close to each other. I could only imagine a rather gloomy and perhaps uncomfortable visit, so decided I would wait till after Finals and make it shortish. In the event, I needn't have worried, that visit was fated never to happen.

But if I had taken the trouble to tell my Dad about Adam ditching me, of course he would have been utterly furious on my behalf and probably quite supportive in his way. Though I knew he would also be rather disappointed that his only daughter had gone in for what he would call 'co-habiting'. He did have rather traditional views. My mother, who had died some years back, would probably have sympathised more with my need for love and affection.

Kate, a friend who had seen me in the library, obviously trying to revise, called round a day or two after Adam had dropped his bombshell. She arrived with a bottle of wine, saying, "Hi

A COMMON THREAD

Gina, you were looking absolutely ghastly the other day, so I was a bit concerned. Are you all right? Not got some bug or other?"

Her eyes widened as she took in this figure huddled in some scruffy pyjamas and an old blanket. I knew my eyes were still red and my face blotchy with weeping, in fact I looked an absolute fright and was obviously still very upset. Then I told her briefly about what had happened. "Did you have a great row about something?" she queried.

I shook my head, "I could have understood it more if we had," I answered. "And before you ask, there was no other person involved, either."

"He does have a bit of a reputation, you know," she said trying to be tactful. I stared wondering if she was telling the truth, trying to make me feel better or was it a dig at me for being a fool.

Nevertheless, I decided to give her some more details. "Adam just told me the other day, quite casually, *Gina, it would be better for both of us if we called it a day. It's been really nice while it lasted, but it's wrong to drift on and perhaps awaken expectations.*

"I wondered at this point if I was hearing things. Surely, he couldn't mean what I thought he had just said. I asked him to think again and wondered if perhaps his work was causing problems or something else like a family matter had upset him. But he said, *Look Gina, my work is ok so are my parents, everything's fine, but it's better and fairer to you to state how I feel.*"

Kate looked at me, "I'll have to tell you what I 've heard about him from quite reliable sources. Our charming popular Adam has apparently done something very like this a time or two at least, not necessarily dropping someone just before Finals, but having close relationships with some young girl for at least say a term or two or longer and then more or less walking away, presumably because he's bored and keen on pastures new. There's a pattern here, a kind of common thread in the way he goes about things. He initiates the whole thing, of course, and is careful always to be the one to finish it. His charm and looks means he knows he can easily find another delighted young woman, proud of her catch. So, you're not the first and maybe not the last; not that that's any real comfort. Course, you're better off without him, but this couldn't come at a worse time."

"Exactly! I feel totally broken up inside, I just can't cope. I just can't think straight. I feel suffocated. It makes sitting my Finals utterly impossible!"

"Don't talk bosh, Gina!" said Kate in outrage. "Are you going to throw away three years hard work, not to mention ruining your life for a self-centred prick? No, you damn well won't. You'll sit your bloody exams and get yourself a damn good degree. Buckle up and bloody well get going. You can come and moan to me occasionally if you must and feel in need of a pep-talk, but for God's sake woman, try to snap out of it."

"Suppose you're right, Kate!" I said wiping my eyes sulkily, inwardly thinking, *I can do without her home truths*. "I'll probably try to put it down to experience, eventually," I continued, somewhat sarcastically, forcing myself to get a grip, but still feeling as if someone had carefully removed a layer of my skin.

"Listen Gina, it really won't be easy, that's an understatement, I know, but you do need to get back your self-respect. It would surely help quite a lot to try to get a damn good degree!"

I went off for a quick wash and tidy up, returning in jeans and sweater while Kate who had found some glasses, poured out

101

the wine she had brought. After making a bit of an effort, I was able to chat to her about her own doings and ask how her revision was going.

Some of her previous words had really struck home.

After she left, I sat musing to myself. A common thread – that's what she'd called it... yet Adam and I really did have some good times in the past... But how utterly naïve I must have been! I smiled bitterly. Yes, no question, I'd been a sitting duck!